CW00828377

IMPORTANT BILLING AND CREDIT REQUIREMENTS

MIXED FEELINGS was first produced at the Civic Theatre, Darlington, May 13, 1987 with the following cast:

ARTHUR VINES .... Brian Murphy
NORMA VINES................................. Ruth Madoc
HAROLD SEDGEWICK.................. Simon Merrick
ROBIN TOOVEY...................... Michael Hammond
SONIA BRADSHAW..................... Sally Knyvette
DENNIS BRADSHAW .... Robin Parkinson

Director.................................... Charles Savage
Designer .... Graham Brown
Lighting Designer........................... Chris Boyle

CHARACTERS

Arthur

Norma

Harold

Sonia

Robin

Dennis

Action takes place during one day.

ACT I

SCENE: Late afternoon. Autumn.

A basement flat. Plain decor enlivened with posters in clip frames mostly of the late 1920's to 1940's mixed with Warhol, Hockney, Rofko, etc. There are one or two plaster busts of 1930 ladies as used in old fashioned haberdashery shops—one wears a military cap. The rest of the furnishings and decor reflect the taste of a fairly successful commercial artist. This is his home and place of work.

The facing wall has book shelves with hi-fi and TV along its length with two doors, both curtained.

From the audience point of view is a door up right leading out to area steps with a glimpse of street railings.

Down right is a recess with a sloping roof made from the ground floor steps to the street. A small bachelor kitchen has been made out of this recess.

Up left is a door to a bedroom and below this are French windows through which we see part of a patio type garden and a large lead Cupid.

There is a desk with a phone and papers and a high Dickensian type clerk's desk which has a drawing board with a half finished design for the jacket of a novel.

An anglepoise above this and there are pots with brushes, pens, spray aerosols, etc.

The rest of the furniture is old but the general effect is harmonious and lived-in.

7

*At this moment the kitchen has a collection of used
pans and dishes, and a saucepan and plates on
the dining table suggest a man living alone.*

*AT RISE: ARTHUR enters from the basement door
with a full bag of washing from the launderette. HIS
face lights up as he sees the winking RED LIGHT
flashing from his answerphone.*

ARTHUR. Ah! (*Goes to it and presses re-wind.*)
Someone out there wants me! (*Goes to area window
and closes venetian blind.*) Do you bring me good
tidings? (*HE returns to the machine and his finger
hovers over the replay button.*) Yes. You look in a jolly
mood! (*HE presses the button and sings a snatch of
"My Blue Heaven" as he takes his washing out and
spreads it around.*)

(*There is a loud dialing tone from the machine, then a
brisk FEMALE VOICE.*)

FEMALE VOICE. Oh, hello, Mr. Vines. This is Dr.
Pitfield's receptionist. Regarding that wisdom tooth
that's been troubling you. Dr. Pitfield has just had a
cancellation so you'll be pleased to know that he can
take it out for you at 2:15 on Tuesday. Will you please
confirm if this is convenient? Thank you.

(*Loud dialing TONE. MALE VOICE is heard.*)

MALE VOICE. Rowlands here. Barclays. I just
wondered, Mr. Vines, if I can look forward to some
funds in the near future to bring your overdraft down
to the agreed limit. Thank you and out.

(*Loud dialing TONE, then a BLEEP sound, then silence.*)

ARTHUR. (*Addressing the answerphone.*) Can't you ever give me good news? Just once! Don't you know what good news is? Aren't you programmed to give good news? (*From his laundry bag he takes out a damp tee shirt and beats the machine with it.*) You miserable little electronic misery guts! Can't you just once, when I come home, give me a nice 'phone message? Something that will give me just a few moments of joy? Why can't you ... when I switch you on ... say ... (*HE goes into a sexy, vaguely American female voice.*) Hi there, Arthur! This is Bo Derek. I just wanna say I think you're the hunkiest man I know and I'm free tonight. (*He goes away muttering as HE continues to sort out his laundry.*) Just something like that. Just once! (*HE takes out a red football jersey.*) ... Mrs. Baldwin has done it again! ... (*HE goes to the phone with the red jersey and dials.*) She's always doing this to me! (*Into phone.*) Mrs. Baldwin. It's Arthur Vines here. I was just sorting out this service wash you did for me. Was that bloke who plays for Arsenal in your launderette today? I've got his football jersey. Well, when he comes to collect his service wash this evening, will you tell him that he's playing for Queen's Park Rangers on Saturday? Why? Because he's got my blue and white jersey. You've found me my string vest? I didn't lose one. You know that? You just found me one. I'll try it for size when I come in next week. (*HE hangs up. An ALARM CLOCK sounds. HE goes over to a tank of tropical fish on the sideboard.*) Good evening, Mavis. Good evening Charles. Dinner time again. I've bought you something brand new tonight. This is real gourmet stuff for Black Widows.

(*HE takes a carton out of his pocket and reads the label.*) Let me tell you what's on the menu tonight! "Snicksnak fish food." Contains everything to keep your pets healthy and alert. Contains Potash ... Nitrogen ... delicious ... *and* freeze-dried maggots. Yum yum. Made in Japan by the Nippon Fish Canning Co. (*Takes off the lid.*) The British can't even produce maggots now ... (*HE takes a sniff and coughs.*) I can't blame them. Don't be greedy, Herman! (*HE takes his cassette which plays the Tannhauser overture on, and goes back to his laundry and gathers it up and throws it on the sofa. HE then notices something. HE takes out a shirt which is white one half and dyed pink the other.*) Oh, Mrs. Baldwin! (*HE goes into the kitchen and collects an old ironing board and iron. HE sets up the ironing board in the middle of the room and stands the iron on it. HE pays out the lead as HE goes to plug it in. The ironing board has begun to sink slowly the moment it was stood up. HE turns and sees it descending. It comes to a halt about fifteen inches from the ground. HE comes over to it. Feels it. It is solid. HE collects a small leather pouffe and places it by the ironing board. HE sits on it and begins to iron a shirt. There it a tap at the door. HE looks up. For a moment HE is unable to locate the sound and turns off the CASSETTE PLAYER. The KNOCK is repeated. HE opens the basement door. HE looks out. HE closes door. As he goes back to his ironing the TAP gets louder and more insistent. HE tracks it down to one of the bookshelf curtains. HE pulls it aside revealing an alcove piled up with assorted junk. Beyond is a door.*)

    ARTHUR. Who's that?
    NORMA. (*Off.*) Me.

ARTHUR. Yes?
NORMA. (*Off.*) Could you open the door?
ARTHUR. Only at grave inconvenience.
NORMA. (*Off.*) Please, Arthur—

(*HE heaves some of the stuff away and opens the door. It can only open about six inches. NORMA's face squeezes into the gap.*)

NORMA. How are you? (*A beat?*) Not sure?
ARTHUR. I'm considering the question. You know I'm slow. What do you want?
NORMA. To discuss something.
ARTHUR. To my benefit?
NORMA. Oh, dear. You're not in one of your moods? Are you pursing your lips? I can't see from here.
ARTHUR. I'm not pursing anything.
NORMA. I need a little help. Will you let me in? I'm beginning to feel like the man in the iron mask.
ARTHUR. Just a moment.

(*HER face disappears as HE starts to pull the boxes away from the door entrance.*)

ARTHUR. Amazing how this stuff accumulates. Must sort it out. (*HE finds a saxophone.*) I'll never play that again for a start! (*HE removes a stuffed eagle.*) Must send this back to Auntie Alice. It's years ago I did that jacket. It was a thriller, I think. "Birds of Prey." (*HE removes a dress maker's dummy which is wearing a fencing outfit and a wire head guard.*) What was that for? Oh, yes. That book on the Olympics. (*HE finds an épée, a plumber's ball cock, various rubber hoses and a Phyllis Dixey type fan, all of which seem to puzzle*) *him.*) Really must sort this out one day! (*As HE tosses them aside, the DOORBELL rings.*) Just a sec. Someone's at my front door.

(*HE opens his basement door. NORMA stands there.*)

NORMA. I thought it'd be easier if I came round the front. (*SHE enters and makes a quick appraisal of the room.*) Why have you barricaded our communicating door?
ARTHUR. I didn't think we had anything left to communicate.

(*HE closes the door. NORMA smiles graciously determined to avoid any unpleasantness.*)

NORMA. Anyway, I daresay all this stuff helps to keep out the draught.
ARTHUR. And the sounds of Mozart's Horn Concerto which you play every evening between six and seven for exactly twenty minutes. Why is it always twenty minutes?
NORMA. I do my workout exercises to it.
ARTHUR. Ah! That's *one* of life's mysteries solved.
NORMA. I'll turn it down
ARTHUR. Thank you.
NORMA. Or I can play a bit from *Aida*. That's got a similar rhythm. If you're bored with Mozart.
ARTHUR. No, please! I don't want *Aida* every night! All that thumping that goes on when the lovers get banged up in the crypt. They sing that song together, don't they? A last farewell to life and love as they die in each other's arms. Oh, no! That'll really

depress me—hearing that every night. So please ... carry on Mozart. I didn't know when I was well off.

NORMA. Oh, look! This is the tent we had when we went on that terrible holiday. (*Gingerly, SHE picks up part of an orange tent.*)

ARTHUR. Which one? Most of them were terrible.

NORMA. You finally found some use for that awful Indian bed-spread? (*SHE indicates the second curtained door.*)

ARTHUR. It keeps the draught out from the bathroom.

NORMA. You've made it very nice down here.

ARTHUR. Bit of a pigsty this evening. (*HE starts to clear the dining table.*)

NORMA. Doing your smalls, are you? (*SHE indicates the ironing board.*) Why is it so low?

ARTHUR. It's missing a bit.

NORMA. I never liked that ironing board.

ARTHUR. It's not very lovable.

NORMA. How are you?

ARTHUR. Not bad. Yourself?

NORMA. Terrible.

ARTHUR. I like your new hair style

NORMA. It's been like this for three months. (*SHE then smiles.*) Thank you anyway. How's work?

ARTHUR. Fine. (*A beat.*) How's yours?

NORMA. Fine.

ARTHUR. I got a card from Juliet. She likes her new job.

NORMA. Yes. I got a card, too. (*SHE beings to do the washing up. There is a pause. Then BOTH go to speak at once.*)

ARTHUR/NORMA. I'm sorry./Sorry.

ARTHUR. I interrupted you.

NORMA. No ... no .. what were you saying?

ARTHUR. How can I help you? Some complaint? Has my Wagner been rattling your teacups?

NORMA. I never hear you. You're as quiet as a mouse down here.

ARTHUR. Shall we talk about the weather? The price of fish? I paid £1.95 for a tiny piece of smoked haddock last week. Is it something about your lesbian Aunt? How is Aunty Gwen?

NORMA. Very well, thank you.

ARTHUR. Oh, good. Is she still with Eunice?

NORMA. Yes. They're still happily living up there in Aberdovey.

ARTHUR. And is Eunice still doing her roadside car maintenance?

NORMA. She's got her own workshop now.

ARTHUR. I wish she'd come and look at my starter motor. And Uncle George is still in the spare room?

NORMA. (*A little emphatic.*) I haven't come down here to discuss Aunty Gwen. It's something we don't talk about in our family.

ARTHUR. I know. I always think that's a pity. I don't think it matters what you do in that department as long as it doesn't frighten the horses.

NORMA. (*Interrupting.*) How is Sonia these days?

ARTHUR. We're still enjoying a mutually satisfying relationship.

NORMA. I thought so. I haven't seen any other ladies come down your area steps.

ARTHUR. No, there's not a lot of glandular activity going on here these days. Well, you get a bit nervous, don't you? All these pamphlets I get through my letter box saying don't do this don't do that! When I shake hands with people now I feel I should wear rubber gloves. What do you want?

NORMA. Your advice.

ARTHUR. My advice? You work for the Citizen's Advice Bureau! You're the expert, not me. You had those three lovely years at Brighton Polytechnic as a mature student. You've got a diploma in problems. Don't ask me for advice. Talk to yourself.

NORMA. I've got a problem which I can only discuss with you. (*SHE comes out from behind the kitchen counter and surveys the ironing board. SHE moves it to the sofa, then wedges the legs against an easy chair, so that the ironing board is now the normal height. SHE puts on one of his shirts to iron.*)

NORMA. (*Stoically.*) I'm very unhappy, Arthur.
ARTHUR. Oh yes?

(*SHE does a ladylike spit on the iron to test it. There is a sizzle. SHE starts ironing.*)

ARTHUR. How can I help you? In the nineteen years we were married you always said that I was the cause of all your unhappiness. For a year we've lived apart, yet you're still unhappy. Is it my presence below you? You want me to sell the flat and move out?

NORMA. It is not you. I've now got used to you being beneath me.

ARTHUR. You must have. As your mother said—I'll always been beneath you. So what d'you want?

NORMA. The day our divorce came through you took me out to dinner and said we would always be part of each other's lives. No matter how many times we married again, we would always have a little corner in our hearts for each other. I've come down to see you this evening because I want to use that corner. I've got myself in a mess and I thought, as you've known me for twenty-two years, you might be kind enough to give me another five minutes to sort me out.

ARTHUR. I'm broke.

NORMA. It's not money.

ARTHUR. Then you've got your five minutes.

NORMA. Thank you. And I haven't troubled you much lately, have I?

ARTHUR. Haven't seen you for ages. Well, if you insist on doing my ironing, I'll finish this book jacket. (*HE goes to his desk, puts on his LAMP and begins to work.*)

(*A slight pause. SHE gives a loud heart felt sign. HE looks up, but does not comment. SHE goes slowly to a table by the French windows where there are some pot plants. SHE picks up a plastic spray and glances out of the window.*)

NORMA. I've been so unhappy lately, that there have been moments when I've wanted to take that garden statue with me to Battersea Bridge, you know? (*SHE turns and tries to give him a bright smile. SHE walks back to the ironing and sprays a shirt.*)

ARTHUR. Not quite. Why, er ... did you want to take that garden statue to Battersea Bridge?

NORMA. I'd have thought that was obvious, Arthur! To tie it round my middle and jump off! (*SHE irons, irritated, then regrets her tone.*) You look surprised?

ARTHUR. I must admit, I didn't think you were thinking of jumping off Battersea Bridge, tied to our lead Cupid. That is news to me. How astonishing!

NORMA. I'm sorry to upset you.

(*During her line HE sharpens a pencil loudly on his electric sharpener.*)

ARTHUR. Pardon?

NORMA. I said I'm sorry to upset you.

ARTHUR. Yes, I'm very surprised, because when I drove past you waiting at the bus stop the other day you looked 28 and quite radiant, standing there in the rain.

NORMA. Why didn't you give me a lift?

ARTHUR. I was going the other way. Why were you going to choose the lead Cupid to tie round you?

NORMA. (*Enunciating patiently.*) To make sure I sunk, of course!

(*ARTHUR TURNS away, back to his work. NORMA pokes her tongue at him behind his back.*)

ARTHUR. Well ...

(*HE turns back to her abruptly and nearly catches her. SHE changes her expression and clears her throat, pats her chest and irons.*)

ARTHUR. I would have been very upset if you *had* jumped off Battersea Bridge with that lead Cupid tied around you.

NORMA. (*Genuinely touched.*) Oh, Arthur! What a lovely thing to say! (*SHE runs to him and kisses him impulsively.*) How nice of you! (*SHE returns to her ironing.*)

ARTHUR. Because half of that lead Cupid is mine.

NORMA. You bastard!

ARTHUR. When we got divorced it was legally agreed you were to have the top two floors of this

house ... (*HE sharpens another pencil.*) I was to have
the basement, but that we would equally share and
enjoy the garden and personally ... (*Resumes work.*)
.. I've always enjoyed looking at that Cupid.

NORMA. (*A tight smile.*) So I should have asked
you permission before I took it?

ARTHUR. That is the law, Norma Jane. And, had
you asked me, I would have been cooperative.

(*HE sprays his work with aerosol fixer.*)

ARTHUR. I would have let you take the garden
roller. It's been out there rusting away for seven years.
It's time someone got some use out of it.

NORMA. That shirt you're wearing smells like those
canals in Venice..

ARTHUR. (*HE sniffs it.*) So it does!.

(*SHE crosses to him with the newly ironed shirt.*)

ARTHUR. How kind. (*HE rises and begins to
change shirts.*)

NORMA. I'll go now. I have an emotional crisis and
all you can do is make fun of me. How can we have
shared all these years and ended up so bankrupt?
(*SHE goes briskly to the door as the shirt is over his
head.*)

ARTHUR. No, dear ... (*HE catches her as SHE
opens the area door.*)

NORMA. Take your hands off me!

ARTHUR. There' s just a few points of order I've
got to raise with you first. (*HE kicks the door shut
behind him and propels her, struggling, to the sofa.*)
First ... *we* are not bankrupt! You have two-thirds of

this house and a third of my income for life unless you re-marry. It's only *me* that's bankrupt.

(*THEY fall back on the sofa together. SHE tries to speak. HE does not allow her.*)

ARTHUR. As for this deep emotional problem you say you have, let me tell you this. (*Still holding her shoulders, HE comes closer on top of her.*) I have known that face of yours since it belonged to an 18-year-old schoolgirl and I can see nothing in it now which gives the slightest hint of any deep emotional disturbance. (*HE rises and goes to the door.*) You've been lying through your teeth since you stepped into this room. I don't know what your game is, but you've come down here to put one over on me and I'm not having it any more! (*HE opens the door.*) The door is open. (*HE adjusts his shirt and goes back to his work, but his composure is ruffled for the first time.*)

NORMA. You're kidding yourself. You've never been any good at sensing my emotions. I've always had to tell you what I was feeling. You could never guess beforehand.

ARTHUR. I once ducked a fraction of a second before you threw a coffee pot at me.

NORMA. I've been unhappy for some time now, Arthur. I tried to put on a bright face, but things got so bad, I had to go to Juliet today and tell her everything. It was her who said I must come to you. Tell Dad everything, she said. He'll sort you out.

(*During this ARTHUR has stopped working. HE rises and closes the door.*)

ARTHUR. I see. Juliet told you to come to me?

NORMA. So you can see it's quite serious.

ARTHUR. For you to have enlisted Juliet's support must have cost you quite an effort.

NORMA. She is Daddy's girl, after all!

ARTHUR. Not at all.

NORMA. She's been taking your side against me for years.

ARTHUR. That's not true. It's just that she's a very balanced, fair-minded young lady. So she thinks I could help you?

NORMA. Yes.

ARTHUR. Trouble is I've had my fingers burnt so often with you. When we divorced I agreed to all your terms because I assumed I was the guilty party. Then I discovered that during our last five years of marriage, you had had four lovers to my one. And one of them was Juliet's boy friend.

NORMA. Ex. She just wanted to stir it up for me.

ARTHUR. Anyway, our daughter now thinks I can help you, so I will listen and give you the benefit of what little wisdom I have. Cup of tea?

NORMA. Yes, please.

(*ARTHUR goes into the kitchen and prepares the tea.*)

NORMA. Six weeks ago my legs gave way. I had to go to bed. Then, equally suddenly, they got better, then suddenly they went floppy again. Dr. Edwards sent me to a psychiatrist who said that floppy legs meant I was trying to escape from reality by retreating to bed.

ARTHUR. That's an interesting change. When we were married it was the reality of the bed you wanted to escape from.

NORMA. (*Passes a hand painfully across her brow.*) Could you be kind to me for just five minutes? (*SHE rises and goes to the window and looks out.*) On my last visit to the psychiatrist, he said he had discovered a pattern in my legs. They were fine when my lover was away, but went floppy when he was coming back. And he's right. My legs have been fine while Harold was away but he's just left a message on the answerphone. He's coming back back tonight and immediately my legs ... oooooh! they've started to go again. (*With bended knees she makes her way back to the sofa and sits just in time.*) Oh, Arthur! They've gone again! Lifeless! Just look! (*SHE waggles them.*)

ARTHUR. They look the same to me.

NORMA. They don't feel as if they belong to me!

ARTHUR. I wish they belonged to Sonia. It's your legs that kept us going so long. I couldn't leave your legs. In fact, it would be no exaggeration to say that for the past five years our marriage ran on your legs.

NORMA. Sonia has got quite nice legs.

ARTHUR. She has. It's just that they are not quite *my* kind of legs.

NORMA. And very shapely hips.

ARTHUR. She has! But if Sonia had your legs and kept her own bum, she need never work again. So what's gone wrong with Harold? I thought everything was hunky dory upstairs. When I last spoke to you—I think it was Juliet's birthday party—you said you couldn't believe such bliss was possible after living with me.

NORMA. Please, Arthur—no jokes. I'm so low. I've just had to have three Valium and four large sherries in order to ...

ARTHUR. (*Then suddenly.*) *Five* lovers!

NORMA. What?

ARTHUR. You've had five lovers to my one.

NORMA. Oh Arthur ... please! This is no time to ...

ARTHUR. I forgot Freddie.

NORMA. I have never had a lover called Freddie.

ARTHUR. Well you didn't deny it in April, dear heart.

NORMA. Freddie?

ARTHUR. I told you I saw him outside on the pavement. (*HE goes to make the tea.*) He woke me up at half past two in the morning when he backed his car against my railings. He was staring at his bumper. Tight as a tick. I thought ... hello? I've seen him before. Then I remembered. He was the judge who decided your maintenance.

NORMA. (*Sighs.*) His name was Ferdie.

ARTHUR. Whatever ... you later had a bit of his legal ad hoc cock! It's no good you looking innocent. Looking round the room like Jack Benny! You had it off with him! But perhaps you've now decided you don't remember Jack Benny?

NORMA. I think I'm getting a little life back into my legs. (*SHE raises delicately and goes carefully to the ironing board and resumes ironing.*) These underpants are a disgrace. I hope you don't have an accident.

ARTHUR. And one night you thumped up and down so much, I heard the coat hangers rattling in your wardrobe. It was snowing outside and for a moment I thought it was Father Christmas and his sleigh bells!

NORMA. Ferdie and I were friends for a tiny, *tiny* time after our divorce He was very kind. He gave me back my self-confidence.

ARTHUR. That night as I watched him lurch back into his Rolls, I thought no wonder he awarded you a third of my salary and the top two floors of this house and awarded me this crummy basement and custody of the rising damp.

NORMA. He was never more than a friendly ship that passed in the night.

ARTHUR. The ship didn't entirely pass. His rear winker light dropped off into my basement. I thought, at the time, that that was about the most I shall ever own of a Rolls Royce—half a rear winker light.

NORMA. Please, Arthur ... (*Closes her eyes wearily.*) Whatever injuries I might have done you, I am paying for them now. I'm in the middle of a nervous breakdown and I've come to you for help.

ARTHUR. Tea bags?

NORMA. Lovely.

ARTHUR. So why this nervous breakdown?

NORMA. The psychiatrist said it was because I couldn't face the truth about myself.

ARTHUR. You've always been a liar and its never bothered you before. You still say you can't remember when it was a penny for the loo or what a half crown looked like. You don't remember that De Gaulle had a big nose. Bertrand Russell you say is some kind of dog and you didn't know Pope John was fat. But Juliet says I must help you, so go on about the psychiatrist.

NORMA. He says my basic trouble is that I can't face the fact that though Harold has lived with me upstairs for eight months, he died, as a lover, six months ago.

ARTHUR. And you hadn't noticed?

NORMA. (*Closes her eyes painfully.*) I couldn't admit it. But I can't run from the truth any more.

ARTHUR. Not with floppy legs.

NORMA. When Harold gets home ... (*Looks at her watch.*) ... in about ten minutes time, I've got to tell him to go. I've already prepared the way by packing his things.

ARTHUR. You've packed Harold's things?!

NORMA. Four cases, a tea chest and two carrier bags.

ARTHUR. You're going to chuck Harold out the moment he gets home?!

NORMA. I have to. Doctor's orders.

ARTHUR. I'm appalled, Norma! (*Throws tea bag in mug.*)

NORMA. I'm not looking forward to it myself!

ARTHUR. Harold left a nice wife in Billericay when he moved in with you. Naturally, I told him not to. I said, in this very room, as your oldest friend, Harold, I must warn you about Norma. Have it off with her by all means. It's all there for the asking ...

NORMA. You've always had these unexpected moments of chivalry.

ARTHUR. ... but whatever you do, don't move in.

NORMA. We were happy but the relationship did not maintain its early promise.

ARTHUR. (*Pouring hot water into the mugs.*) Why did he never listen to me? I am not pleased, Norma!

NORMA. Do you think I am? My nerves are twitching all over, my legs have gone, I look a hundred. I'm at my lowest ebb! (*A little sob.*) That's why I've come to you. As he's your oldest friend, will *you* tell him he's got to go?

(*A pause while HE stares at her in disbelief poised with the sugar. SHE moves to the kitchen as SHE gathers up the underpants.*)

ARTHUR. Me?

NORMA. Yes.

ARTHUR. You've actually come down here to ask *me* to give your lover the elbow?

NORMA. Because he's your oldest friend and it'll sound much nicer coming from you. It's the kindest way of getting rid of him says Juliet and I agreed. We thought you could tell him when he comes down with that whisky he always bring you back from America. (*Sips her tea.*)

ARTHUR. You want me to say thanks for the Southern Comfort, Harold, but your bags are packed because Norma finds you a pain in the arse?

NORMA. Do you have to be so low?

ARTHUR. Your bags are packed because you get on Norma's tits?

NORMA. Our daughter thought that the nicest thing to say was that my legs have gone floppy because I couldn't face the awful truth that I was still in love with my ex-husband.

ARTHUR. Who?

NORMA. You. And Harold will believe that—if *you* tell him.

ARTHUR. (*Steely.*) Why will he believe it, Norma?

NORMA. Because he knows you would never lie to him. He'd be much happier about leaving then.

ARTHUR. He would?

NORMA. Because he'd know it wasn't his fault. He wasn't being rejected for a new lover, it's just that I had failed to get *you* out of my system.

ARTHUR. (*Points to the door.*) Kindly vacate these premises.

NORMA. (*Slightly unnerved.*) He will believe it, if you tell him, Arthur. He's always suspected I'm still carrying a torch for you.

(*ARTHUR strides to the ironing board, wrenches a shirt from Norma and begins to stuff all the laundry back into the bag.*)

ARTHUR. Well I must put Harold straight on that immediately. When he comes down here I shall tell him that if Norma is still carrying a torch for me, it's only because one day she hopes to set light to me with it!

NORMA. You don't have to say you return my feelings ...

ARTHUR. Out! (*HE hurls the bag of washing into the bedroom then unplugs the iron.*)

NORMA. You can say we will never live together again ...

ARTHUR. I am saying nothing to nobody! (*Burns his hand on the iron.*) Shit!

NORMA. You can tell him I'm going mad—anything! Just so long as you make it nice for him.

(*ARTHUR grabs the ironing board and throws it in the kitchen cupboard.*)

NORMA. And I do want to make it nice for him.

(*The cupboard door flies open and an assortment of cleaning equipment falls out with the ironing board. With muttered grunts and swearing, ARTHUR rams everything back in. Slams door. Waits. HE takes a pace away. The door flies open. HE bangs it shut. Turns away. Takes a pace. Turns back abruptly. Door remains closed.*)

NORMA. It's not his fault I can't love him anymore and I know I never shall.

(*This remark diverts him from the cupboard.*)

ARTHUR. You don't know that. How can you know that?

NORMA. Because I now notice the way he blows his nose then looks in his hanky. I am very unhappy, Arthur! And Harold will believe you. He knows you went off me first.

ARTHUR. That is all LIES! (*HE bangs the kitchen counter and the cupboard door swings open. HE leaps to it and bangs it shut.*)

NORMA. You stopped fancying me on the 20th June three years ago. It was a Thursday.

ARTHUR. I stopped fancying you?

NORMA. That night you said that if I wanted to keep your interest I must adopt bizarre positions! (*Sips tea.*)

ARTHUR. Bizarre! All I ever asked for was a slight variation from you just lying there and counting the cobwebs on the ceiling!

NORMA. What a dreadful thing to say!

ARTHUR. I once heard you count up to eight!

NORMA. That's not true!

ARTHUR. I was making love to you one summer evening and you counted the cobwebs aloud!

NORMA. I may have counted the cobwebs, but I never counted eight! I would never have had enough time, for one thing. (*Sips tea.*)

ARTHUR. (*Strides furiously through the gap in the counter.*) You shouldn't have been counting *any* cobwebs! (*HE angrily bangs the counter flap down.*)

(*The cupboard door bursts open. Everything falls out
      but he is now the wrong side of the counter and
      cannot reach it. The final cannister of polish falls
      out.*)

NORMA. I've never said housework was my forte.

(*A TAXI is heard arriving. NORMA leaps to the window
      and peers up round the edge of the blind.*)

NORMA. Oh God! It's him! Horrible Harold! He's
arrived! (*Growing panic.*) Arthur ... please ... don't
desert me now. I beg you. Just this one last favor!
You've lived down here a year now and I haven't been
any trouble, have I? I've never interfered with your life.
You talk about me and Ferdie and the coat hangers.
Last week I heard this terrible squawking down here. I
thought it was a trapped chicken for a moment, then I
realized it was Sonia. She went on and on simulating a
most unlikely degree of ecstasy ...
      ARTHUR. How dare you!
      NORMA. But I didn't interfere. I didn't bang on the
ceiling. I was reading *Little Dorrit* at the time. I had to
read the same page twice but I didn't complain. I want
you to be happy. (*Runs back and looks up through
the window.*) And I just thought—for the sake of our
twenty years together and our lovely daughter,— he's
paying the taxi—you 'd tell him this little white lie and
then I'll come down and confirm it and say how sorry I
am. (*SHE runs up to the window again.*) He looks as
appetizing as a ton of condemned sausage meat.
Whatever did I see in him! (*Runs back to Arthur taking
out some paper from her skirt pocket.*) Now I've typed
out a few notes about what to say ...
      ARTHUR. You've written me a speech?

NORMA. No ... no ... just a few points about how peculiar I've become and then say ... (*Reads.*) ... about my happy legs ... what? Where's your glasses? (*SHE gets them from the desk and reads.*) Floppy legs ... and say that because I've tried to deny my true feelings the conflict has gone to my legs.

ARTHUR. (*HE takes the paper and is suddenly very calm.*) Have you ever noticed, Norma, that whenever you had any dirty work to do, I always had to do it? When you didn't want your Aunty Beryl living with us any more, *I* had to tell her. I loved her living with us. All those Nellie Wallace songs she used to sing. (*Slowly HE begins to tear up the note letting the bits drop into a crowded waste-paper basket.*) She hated that old peoples' home and just before she died there, she said to me she forgave me for throwing her out. Forgave *me!* But now, Norma dear, the time has come for you to do your own dirty work. For the good of your soul you are going to tell Harold the truth about yourself. You're going to tell him face to face why you are chucking him out. I strongly suspect it's because you've found a new Mr. Wonderful but you don't want to tell him that because there might be ructions. Anyway, baby, this one is on you! (*HE calmly sits at his desk and begins to work.*)

(*DOORBELL. NORMA gets a packet of cornflakes from the kitchen counter and on her way to the center door, SHE rams the box down on his head. NORMA scrambles over the debris to make her exit through the middle door.*)

ARTHUR. And you'd better tell him the truth, my cherub, because if he asks me, I will. And the truth is, Harold, she hates my guts.

(*As SHE scrambles through the door, SHE turns and
    gives him a V sign.*)

ARTHUR. You're not pissing over me anymore!
You two-faced, devious Welsh pit pony!

(*SHE gives him the finger sign. Exits. The door
    SLAMS and HE piles back the rubbish. HE opens
    his front door.
HAROLD steps in carrying a suitcase and a small grip.
    HE is a well built man in his late 40's with a face
    which exudes integrity and obvious
    dependability.*)

HAROLD. You've got your head in a box of
cornflakes.

(*ARTHUR goes to remove it and the cornflakes
    cascade over his face making his reply
    incoherent.*)

HAROLD. You don't have to explain. You're an
artist. A law unto yourself.

(*ARTHUR puts packet in waste-paper basket and
    removes the remaining flakes on his head and in
    his shirt.*)

HAROLD. Perhaps you're designing the jacket for
some book on ancient Egypt? (*HE glances at the
drawing board.*)
    ARTHUR. No. Why?
    HAROLD. When you answered the door you
looked exactly like Ramses the second. (*H E*

free bag.) I bring comfort and joy from Bogota. Plus twenty-five Monte Cristos. (*Takes out cigar box*.)

ARTHUR. My dear Harold! (*Takes bottle with a slightly embarrassed smile.*) Once more the traveller returns with gifts! How wonderful! What can I say? What can I do? (*ARTHUR seems rooted to the spot as HE stares at him.*)

HAROLD. Open it for a start. Or aren't I going to get my customary welcome home snifter?

ARTHUR. Of course! What am I thinking of? (*HE goes into the kitchen, puts the bottle on the counter, kicks aside the hidden debris and finds two glasses.*) You're home early, aren't you? (*Hastily.*) I don't know why I said that. No one told me when you were due home. I know nothing about anything ... Did you do some good deals? (*Smiles with bonhomie as HE nervously opens the bottle.*)

HAROLD. You're quite right, though. I am early. We had tail winds over the Azores.

ARTHUR. That was nice. And the trip was fruitful?

HAROLD. Couldn't put a foot wrong. Mind you, September, has always been my lucky month. I was born with Mercury in Uranus.

ARTHUR. (*Distracted as HE pours the drinks.*) Mercury in your what?

HAROLD. My star sign. That's why things always turn out well for me in September.

ARTHUR. Oh good. I hope it continues. (*Swigs a drink.*)

HAROLD. I'm treading these cornflakes into your shag pile. I'll shake it out for the birds.

ARTHUR. Don't bother. How was Caracas?

HAROLD. (*Carefully gathers up the rug.*) No idea.

ARTHUR. You've just been there.

HAROLD. Bogota.

ARTHUR. How was Bogota?

HAROLD. Well, it's no Caracas.

ARTHUR. Why not?

HAROLD. Caracas is low. Bogota is high. (*Takes rug to French windows.*) Which makes your pulse go twenty beats above normal. (*Shakes out the rug on the patio.*) The majority of the population has amoebic dysentery.(*ARTHUR refills his glass.*) The rivers are full of Piranha fish and they have poisonous spiders which jump out on you and their bite kills you within twenty minutes. But they've got something even worse in Peru where I went last March.

ARTHUR. What have they got in Peru?

HAROLD. (*Still with his back to Arthur, is now carefully picking out the remaining cornflakes from the shag pile.*) A tick which lives in the rivers, and if you go for a swim, it crawls up the male member and once it's there, the only way you can survive is to amputate it.

ARTHUR. I don't think I'll be going there for my holidays.

(*HAROLD returns with the rug.*)

ARTHUR. I mean you don't mind leaving your heart in San Francisco but you don't want to leave your member in Peru!

HAROLD. (*Spreading the rug.*) And when I was in Madagascar last year ...

ARTHUR. Don't tell me. Have a drink. (*HE gets the two glasses.*)

HAROLD. I tell you, Arthur, I've been all over the world building bridges, and every time I come home, I thank God for Fulham Broadway! (*Takes glass.*) Cheers!

ARTHUR. Cheers!

HAROLD. So how's things with you? (*HE goes up to the drawing board and stares at the book jacket design.*) Another book jacket?

ARTHUR. A medical book about schizophrenia.

HAROLD. Why have you drawn a woman in the foreground and this funny looking woman behind her?

ARTHUR. Well, that's the disease. You're never alone with schizophrenia.

HAROLD. How's Sonia?

ARTHUR. She's fine.

HAROLD. She's still bringing you your weekly food parcels and a selection from her old man's wine cellar?

ARTHUR. Oh, yes! Same old routine.

HAROLD. If her husband ever finds out that for the past two years you've not only been sleeping with his wife every Friday, but he's also supplied the booze and the grub, which will annoy him most? (*Chuckles.*) Conjures up quite a humorous picture, don't you think?

ARTHUR. I can think of funnier pictures.

HAROLD. What did she bring you last week?

ARTHUR. A game pie and two bottles of Chateau Lafitte.

HAROLD. And he hasn't noticed so far?

ARTHUR. No.

HAROLD. I daresay the Chairman of Incorporated Chemicals has got enough to do without checking his wine cellar.

ARTHUR. Well, I'd better get on. (*HE makes a very obvious effort at working.*)

HAROLD. May I hoover up these cornflakes?

ARTHUR. Don't bother, Harold.

HAROLD. They worry me.

ARTHUR. No please ... anyway I don't have a Hoover, just a Ewbank.

HAROLD. What's the difference?

ARTHUR. Mine's thinner and quieter and needs pushing. But please don't ...

HAROLD. (*Goes into the kitchen.*) My pleasure! I say! What a mess! (*HE takes his coat off.*)

ARTHUR. Please don't trouble yourself, Harold ...

HAROLD. No trouble. I love doing these domestic things after two weeks in a tropical rain forest. (*HE sings quietly to himself as HE rolls up his sleeves.*)

(*PHONE rings.*)

ARTHUR. (*Into phone.*) Hello? (*His tone becomes instantly wary.*) Oh hello, Juliet. Yes I know Mum came to see you. (*HE glances at Harold and turns away from him.*) Yes. I have had a meeting with a lady and we had a frank exchange of views. Er ... well ... both parties made candid statements about their respective positions. No, a further meeting is not envisaged in the near future. Er ... no, it's not the ideal moment.

(*HAROLD disappears under the counter. ARTHUR is puzzled. HE stands up on a rung of his high stool to see what Harold is doing.*
HAROLD's hand appears with a brush which HE puts on the counter and continues with other similar items, such as cleaning rags, cannisters, electrical appliances, tins of soup, baked beans etc.)

ARTHUR. Yes, I know she hates herself for doing it, but I will hate myself even more if *I* do it. (*His voice is low and urgent.*) I know she's upset. I know she just can't help herself. But he's my oldest ...

(*HAROLD appears and puts the ironing board in the cupboard.*)

ARTHUR. ...uncle. Uncle *Norman* , you know?

(*HAROLD closes the door. It swings open again.*)

ARTHUR. I spoke to *him* tonight ... Uncle *Norman* ... well, I told him straight. He was old enough to sort out his own boyfriends. What?

(*HAROLD examines the door hinges of the cupboard and gets a screwdriver from a drawer.*)

ARTHUR. Of course I meant girl friends. You nit picker.

(*HAROLD steps into the cupboard.*)

ARTHUR. (*Suddenly low and furtive.*) He's here now. In the broom cupboard. I can't go into details. I see. I see. You sound very convinced. M'mm ... I might. I can't promise you anything.

(*HAROLD comes out of the cupboard.*)

ARTHUR. I'll be over for supper on Monday as usual.

(*HAROLD shuts door. It remains shut.*)

ARTHUR. I haven't decided. Bye bye, darling. (*HE hangs up. Resumes work.*)

(*HAROLD gets the Ewbank, comes out of the kitchen
and begins to sweep up the cornflakes.
ARTHUR eyes HAROLD as HE sings a snatch of "Trial
by Jury."*)

HAROLD. (*Sings.*) When I, good friends, was called to the bar ... with an appetite fresh and hearty ...

ARTHUR. (*Rises and crosses to the window.*) Why am I doing this, Harold?

HAROLD. I'm sorry? (*Stops sweeping.*)

ARTHUR. Is it the memory of when Norma and I were in our twenties? When I had hair and she didn't have hot flushes? Is it because I remember when we lived in one room in Shepherds Bush and I came home one day and Norma was standing there—so pregnant. "The water's broke," she said, and I saw her wet slippers and pretended to keep calm. Her dad had given us his 1948 Morris. It had L plates. Norma was teaching me to drive. So slowly, but trying to be quick, we drove to the hospital and we joked about me being the learner and I had to be accompanied by a qualified driver— which was Norma. As they took her off on a stretcher, she said how would I get back? And we laughed because we were frightened and I drove back on my own. But I got too close to a line of parked cars. Somehow I couldn't steer away and very, very slowly I knocked off six wing mirrors. I got home and that night Juliet was born. Is that why?

HAROLD. I'm not quite ...

ARTHUR. We've always played the game with each other, haven't we, Harold? Ever since our National Service in the Catering Corps, we've always played the game.

HAROLD. Is something amiss, Arthur?

ARTHUR. You and I are such old friends. Must be thirty years. You were my best man. All three of us are such old friends. When Norma and I called it a day, I was so pleased you took up with her ... you being such an old mate. I congratulated you didn't I?

HAROLD. Well actually, you said I needed my head examined.

ARTHUR. I did?

HAROLD. I think you tried to put me off because you didn't think it would work out.

ARTHUR. That's right.

HAROLD. You thought one of us would get hurt.

ARTHUR. Exactly.

HAROLD. And the hurt would be so much more painful because we've all been such good friends for so long.

ARTHUR. Precisely, I didn't want to risk losing such old friends as you and Norma. I shall always love Norma, in my funny way. I shall always love you, Harold, in my funny way.

HAROLD. I feel the same, Arthur.

ARTHUR. I shall never find another friend like you, Harold.

HAROLD. Ditto. Ditto.

ARTHUR. When you're young it's no problem, but at our age ...

HAROLD. We don't have the commitment. We've made our friends at a certain point in our lives and can't make any more.

ARTHUR. Absolutely. But I should have gone before today.

HAROLD. Are you going somewhere now?

ARTHUR. We are parting ... yes, Harold.

HAROLD. You haven't got ...? That trouble you had downstairs hasn't got worse? The shingles on your ...?

ARTHUR. No that's cleared up nicely, thank you, but actually there is a medical problem—Norma's.

HAROLD. She hasn't caught it? Perhaps I've got it now.

ARTHUR. No—with Norma it's mental.

HAROLD. Mental?

ARTHUR. For some months now, unbeknown to me, she's been under a psychiatrist. He phoned me today and said Norma was losing her marbles. He used words like paranoic inversion causing a locomotive trauma which means the same thing. She's going barmy.

HAROLD. She didn't look barmy when I left nine days ago. I thought how lovely and serene she looked.

ARTHUR. That's a front. You get that with psychosomatic symbolic syndromes. It's well known.

HAROLD. But what's the cause of all this?

ARTHUR. (*Takes a breath.*) She doesn't know why she can't get me out of her system ... (*HE turns to the window and rolls his eyes.*) and the problem has given her a nervous breakdown. It would, of course. It's inexplicable. Women have been giving me elbow since I was 12 and they've never given it a second thought. So why Norma can't get over me is as mysterious as the riddle of why you always have 21 socks in your drawer and none of them match.

HAROLD. I see. (*HE absently takes up the Ewbank again.*) Yes. I get you. (*Sweeps.*) Oh dear. (*Sweeps.*) Yes, I do see. (*Stops.*) You and Norma are going to live together again?

ARTHUR. I wouldn't live with Norma for a thousand pounds a day paid in used notes into a Swiss bank account. It's not *me* that's going barmy. This is her problem entirely.

HAROLD. So what's she going to do? Has she spoken to you about it?

ARTHUR. Yes.

HAROLD. What did she say?

ARTHUR. Well ... she says ... (*HE goes blank then puts on his glasses and empties the waste-paper basket on the table.*) Excuse me. I've just lost a check. Just occurred to me I might have torn it up by mistake. I can't concentrate till I find it. (*HE sorts through the scraps of paper.*) Ah! (*HE reads a fragment of note paper.*) Yes ... she says she despises herself for feeling ... (*HE puts segment of paper to one side and rummages through the rest.*) For feeling ... (*HE discards some pieces of paper, then finds another piece.*) ... got it! That it's not that she doesn't love you, Harold.

HAROLD. Yes?

ARTHUR. (*Frowns at the paper.*) But she loves me better. No, I'm adrift there. The thing is, Harold, this ... this (*Finds another piece.*) lunatic obsession she's got about me has set up a conflict which has gone ... (*Reads another scrap.*) someway towards settling your over-draft ... no, as you were, Harold ... (*He busks from now on.*) Anyway, I said to her, Norma. Norma, I said. How can you still fancy me? You know what a dog's life I led you, like when you came home unexpectedly and found Sonia naked in the wardrobe. Did I ever tell you that, Harold? Norma came in, saw me pretending to be asleep in bed. Then went straight to the wardrobe, opened it and said, "Oh, it's only you, Sonia," and closed the door. Sonia was furious.

HAROLD. So what's my position?

ARTHUR. I'll get Norma. (*Dials phone.*) Done my bit. What I mean is, Harold ... it all boiled up while you were away, you see? (*Into phone.*) Please come down. You can use my door. Yes, I've told Harold everything. What? No. You can tell him yourself about the floppy legs. (*HE hangs up and opens the curtain and once more begins to clear a passage.*)

HAROLD. Floppy legs?

ARTHUR. The doctor says she's got these funny legs because she's been denying her true feelings, but Norma will tell you all the details. (*HE opens the door and calls up.*) We're waiting, Norma. (*Turns back.*) So that's your position.

HAROLD. What is?

ARTHUR. Well, she's got this crisis and you are the only one who can help her.

HAROLD. How?

ARTHUR. How? By giving her a chance to sort herself out.

HAROLD. How do I do that?

ARTHUR. Well ... er ... you know ... by sort of ... leaving.

HAROLD. Leaving! Leaving!

(*HE comes to ARTHUR who backs anxiously.*)

ARTHUR. Only then will she realize how much she needs you. (*Yanks open the middle door.*) Where the hell ...?

(*NORMA is outside and has obviously been listening. SHE straightens up and enters with as much dignity as the various obstacles permit. SHE is wearing a somber dress.*)

NORMA. Hello, Harold. It's nice to see you back safe and sound. (*SHE smiles at him with a gracious sympathy, then glares at Arthur in angry hurt.*) How *could* you, Arthur?

ARTHUR. How could I what?

NORMA. You had no right at all to tell Harold anything! When we discussed it, I told you I was going to tell Harold myself. It was my duty to tell him. (*To Harold.*) But I would never have told you, Harold, the moment you walked into the house. I do apologize for Arthur's behavior! (*To Arthur.*) You've actually told him what the psychiatrist has said?

ARTHUR. (*Slowly threatening.*) Yes, Norma ... I've told Harold what he has to do to solve your crisis. I told him because I thought you had reached your limit. We all have limits. There's only so much I can take, then *I* get a crisis.

NORMA. (*Takes hint.*) Yes ... quite. Well, Harold, now that Arthur has told you, what more can I say? I'm still in love with Arthur and I hate myself for it.

HAROLD. You've felt like this for some time?

NORMA. But it's nothing to do with you. It's not your fault I can't get Arthur out of my system.

(*During this, ARTHUR has gone up to the table behind Harold and is scooping the paper back into the waste-paper basket.*)

NORMA. We can't stand each other and I despise myself for feeling as I do but I just can't help it. Inside me there is this terrible ... (*Tries to remember.*) terrible er ...

ARTHUR. (*ARTHUR finds a piece of her note. Prompts her quietly.*) Conviction!

NORMA. (*Loudly.*) Conviction! Got it! Yes! Conviction that I am incapable of loving another man. The doctor said that I have to face up to the awful truth that I am a ... (*Forgets.*) Shit! (*Stamps foot.*)

(*ARTHUR empties the entire waste-paper basket back onto the table and searches.*)

ARTHUR. One m ...

NORMA. (*Suddenly remembers.*) One-man woman! I've tried so hard to get over him, Harold it has set up an inner ... (*Arthur waits—not sure if he'll be needed again.*) ... upheaval ... no ... turmoil ... no ... disturbance ... er not quite ...

ARTHUR. (*Rummages again.*) Conflict.

NORMA. (*Leaping onto it loudly.*) Conflict! Conflict! Yes ... an inner conflict which has gone straight to my legs. My mind is reeling. I'm going totally hysterical. I have tried to get over him, Harold. Please believe me.

HAROLD. (*Takes out hanky.*) I do. Of course I do, darling.

(*SHE sniffs. HAROLD offers her his hanky.*)

NORMA. (*Shakes her head.*) But I never meant to tell you the moment you came home.

HAROLD. No. No. (*Carefully arranges hanky to blow in.*) So you'd like me to leave in the near future, Arthur?

ARTHUR. Well it's not entirely me. (*Appeals to Norma to take over.*) Norma?

NORMA. No, really, Arthur. Don't beat about the bush anymore. Tell him about his cases.

ARTHUR. (*Exploding.*) I am not going to tell him they've been packed and that's final!

HAROLD. You've actually packed my cases, Arthur! Well that's it. Finito!

(*As HAROLD stares fixedly into his hanky, ARTHUR kicks her behind and SHE immediately back tracks.*)

NORMA. No, Harold, you mustn't blame Arthur entirely. I am the one who is awful and ... oh dear, Harold ... you've been so lovely to me ...

(*SHE goes to fling her arms round his neck but HE blows his nose loudly.*
SHE amends her imploring gesture to adjusting her earrings and turning away as HE looks into his hanky.)

NORMA. So lovely! Believe me, Harold, I've never hated myself so much as I do at this moment.

HAROLD. I'm sorry I haven't managed to woo you from the old bastard. (*Gives small smile to Arthur.*) I do understand, Norma. Don't blame yourself.

NORMA. (*Turning back to him.*) Oh, how wonderful you ... (*Sees him still staring into the hanky and turns back immediately.*) ...you are, Harold.

HAROLD. I mean it. You mustn't punish yourself.

NORMA. I won't then.

HAROLD. No point in getting passionate — not now that Arthur has packed my bags.

ARTHUR. (*Glares at Norma.*) I er ...

HAROLD. Don't deny it, Arthur. We've always played the game with each other. You want me to go, so I'm dead. How many cases did you pack?

NORMA. (*Quickly.*) Well there's the one you've got there and four more upstairs, two carrier bags and a tea chest with your books and your *Salmon and Trout* magazines.

HAROLD. And a tea chest!

NORMA. And two little fishing rods.

HAROLD. What about my landing net?

NORMA. What's it look like?

ARTHUR. Like a snood on a stick.

NORMA. What's a snood?

ARTHUR. A string bag for your hair. You remember! Women used to wear them in the war.

HAROLD. Long before Norma's time.

NORMA. Thank you, Harold. (*Gives a steely look to Arthur.*) Yes. That's there, too.

HAROLD. I can't take that lot to a hotel. I'd better give the wife a tinkle. She'll be surprised. Only last month I popped back to collect my golf clubs and told Hermione how happy I was here.

ARTHUR. Where's his golf clubs?

HAROLD. At the club. There's a very good pair of waterproof shoes under the sink.

NORMA. They're nicely wrapped in the tea chest.

HAROLD. So I've got everything?

NORMA. Yes.

HAROLD. If only I had. I've been so comfortable upstairs with you, Norma. Your wonderful salad dressing. Still ... you know what they say? (*Forgets.*) I had it a minute ago.

NORMA. Oh yes! How very true! I had it a minute ago.

HAROLD. What? No ... (*Remembers.*) Oh yes ... "Over every secure life, boredom hangs like a bird of prey." (*HAROLD sits and puts box of cigars back into his grip.*)

NORMA. I am so dreadful sorry I've let you down. When Arthur rejected me, Harold, I shall never forget how you came along and helped me pick up the pieces.

HAROLD. Thing is, Norma ... O.k. ... you're going through some kind of mental crisis and your doctor says you'll only get better if I move out.

NORMA. So he says.

HAROLD. But if Arthur doesn't want to live with you again ...?

ARTHUR. And I don't. I want that entered into the minutes.

HAROLD.... how can my leaving make you better? (*Pause.*) Perhaps you feel that if you can't have Arthur, you'd rather have nobody?

NORMA. (*Leaping on this.*) That's it! In a nut shell!

HAROLD. But isn't that humiliating? To keep wanting someone who doesn't want you?

NORMA. It is! Dreadful! How can I humiliate myself like this? Everyone says that. ... my mother, my friends. Sonia thinks I'm pathetic, doesn't she, Arthur?

ARTHUR. (*Not looking up from his drawing.*) She does.

NORMA. She said, "You know Arthur despises you!"

ARTHUR. Absolutely.

NORMA. "You must be off your rocker," she said.

ARTHUR. You're making yourself a laughing stock.

NORMA. Her exact words. But the moment I sort myself out, I will let you know, Harold. If there's anything to let you know, I will let you know it.

HAROLD. (*Rises.*) I don't have to take all my belongings now, do I? If I arrive at Hermione's with five cases, a grip, three carrier bags, a tea chest and my fishing tackle she might have one of her funny turns.

NORMA. Of course. Take a couple of cases now and see how the land lies.

(*A DOORBELL is heard downstairs.*)

NORMA. That's my bell.

HAROLD. It's probably Robin from the office with some papers. I said I'd be home about now. Perhaps he'd give me a lift to Billericay.

NORMA. I'll ask him. Oh ... dear Harold. (*SHE kisses him on the forehead and exits with a smothered sob.*)

HAROLD. I suppose I should have seen this coming. She was a bit strange last month when I got back from Botswana. Even so, I must admit ... it's a bit sudden.

ARTHUR. Very sorry, Harold. I feel quite sullied by the whole business. You haven't even got a bed for the night.

HAROLD. Except with my wife and her fifteen goats.

ARTHUR. Yes, there's always Hermione.

HAROLD. And she's always 16 stone. I don't suppose Sonia was very pleased when Norma told her how she felt about you.

ARTHUR. No, but she's known for some time Norma was going peculiar.

HAROLD. Women are so much better at reading the signs.

(*There is a discreet tap at the door and NORMA enters.*)

NORMA. (*A hushed, sympathetic tone.*) Excuse me, Harold. It is someone from your office. Do come down, Mr. Turvey.

(*ROBIN, a fresh-faced young man, appears tentatively at the doorway.*)

ROBIN. It's Toovey, actually, Mrs. Vines.
NORMA. So sorry.
ROBIN. Evening, Harold. Good trip?
HAROLD. Fine.
ROBIN. I can give you a lift to Billericay.
HAROLD. Thanks. This is my assistant, Robin. Arthur.
ARTHUR. Hello.
ROBIN. Nice to meet you.
HAROLD. Sorry to be a nuisance, Robin.
ROBIN. My pleasure.
NORMA. You get your license back next month, Harold, so that'll be something to look forward to, won't it?
HAROLD. Put two of the bags upstairs in your car will you, Robin?
ROBIN. Will do. Good night.
ARTHUR. Good night.

(*ROBIN goes.*)

NORMA. I'll just see you out. (*Goes through the door and then puts her head round the the corner.*) You can leave the front door key with Arthur. (*SHE beams and exits closing the door.*)
HAROLD. Well it's me back to Hermione's. Not the homecoming I imagined when I was sipping champagne in the jumbo but ... (*Takes out some keys*

and removes two from the ring.) everyone seems to want me to go at once, if not sooner, so I'll love you and leave you. (*Puts keys on the table.*) Ah, well ... a wise man embraces adversity. (*Picks up his bags.*) As some idiot once said.

(*ARTHUR opens his front door and HAROLD exits.
ARTHUR remains there a moment looking up and listening to voices.
CAR DOOR slams. A beat. CAR drives off.
ARTHUR closes door and goes back to his drawing board.
The middle door opens a little and NORMA peeps in.*)

NORMA. Oh, Arthur! He's actually gone! (*Embraces Arthur from behind and kisses the back of his head.*) Thank you. I'll tidy you up a bit. That's the least I can do. (*SHE sings quietly to herself as SHE tidies the room.*) You got rid of him with the minimum of fuss and embarrassment, just as Juliet said you would. Harold is your oldest friend, and yet you did it for me!

ARTHUR. I did it because Juliet phoned and said I should. You were genuinely deeply unhappy. I'm sorry I doubted you.

NORMA. That's all right.

ARTHUR. How's your legs?

NORMA. Getting stronger by the minute.

(*Front door opens. SONIA enters carrying groceries and a business-like over-night case. SHE is a pretty, fairish woman of about 40- with an alert, springy step in her walk. SHE wears a discreetly expensive suit.*)

SONIA. Hello, darling. Had a good week? There's some heavy things in the car. Will you be a love and get them? (*SHE crosses to kiss Arthur at his drawing board, then freezes as SHE sees Norma in the kitchen.*) Oh! Hello, Norma.

NORMA. (*Hastily, genuinely nervous.*) Hello, Sonia. I'm just going. Just popped down to have a chat to Arthur about Juliet our daughter.

SONIA. I know who Juliet is.

NORMA. Of course. I'm just going. Anyway, Arthur I'll er ... tell her about ... your feelings in the matter.

ARTHUR. Please yourself. (*Exits front door.*)

SONIA. Sorry to have disturbed you.

NORMA. No, no ... we have finished. I was on my way.

(*SHE scrambles and squeezes over the obstacles in the alcove of the middle door in her effort to make a quick exit.*
SHE gets stuck. SONIA doesn't move to help her.)

NORMA. Been terrible weather for September hasn't it?

SONIA. Yes.

NORMA. I love your boots.

SONIA. Thank you.

NORMA. If I come back in the next life, I shall marry a rich man.

SONIA. Actually I buy all my clothes out of my own earnings.

NORMA. So sorry. Do beg your pardon.

SONIA. (*Appears to soften.*) That a new dress? It's pretty.

NORMA. (*Surprised and pleased.*) Oh! Thank you very much. Yes. I bought it last week. It was very reasonable.

SONIA. Was it one week's alimony or two?

NORMA. I'll pop back up then. Nice to have met you again, Sonia. Long time no see.

(*NORMA exits and SONIA immediately and furiously piles all the boxes back so that the door is totally blocked as at the opening. Finally, SHE draws the curtain across with a passionate venom.*
ARTHUR enters carrying a cardboard box of food, wine, etc. HE is relieved to see NORMA has gone.)

ARTHUR. Had a very good week?

SONIA. Excellent till today.

(*ARTHUR decides not to pursue this and hums to himself as he takes the box to the kitchen.*)

SONIA. I'll do that.

ARTHUR. Right. I'll just finish off my doings here. (*HE sits at his drawing board and works.*)

(*SHE eyes him for a moment but HE continues to hum blithely.*)

SONIA. I have to tell you, Arthur, seeing Norma down here does not please me.

ARTHUR. Nor me.

SONIA. (*Goes down to the kitchen and unpacks the box. Bangs a bottle down.*) What's wrong with Juliet?

ARTHUR. Nothing. Norma thinks she's about to move in with an unsuitable boyfriend.

SONIA. But only Norma thinks he's unsuitable?

ARTHUR. Exactly. There's no problem. I'll sort it out. I say! I'm doing well this week! Side of smoke salmon, a whole salami ... is all this on your husband's account at Harrods?

SONIA. No. His account at Fortnum's. (*Opens his fridge.*) The fridge is empty!

ARTHUR. Yes. But last week's lot lasted till lunch time today.

SONIA. There's nothing in here but ice cubes and a light bulb.

ARTHUR. I know. If you hadn't arrived in time I was going to have them for my supper.

(*HE crosses over to her. THEY kiss with the kitchen counter between them.*)

ARTHUR. And what delights have you brought me from his cellar? (*Examines the bottles.*) Gevrey Chambertin '72 ... very acceptable. A '68 Volnay ... that'll go down well.

SONIA. What's different about you from when I saw you last Friday?

ARTHUR. I'm a week older.

SONIA. No. Your hair.

ARTHUR. Mrs. McNab in the pet shop gave me a haircut. She often gives me a trim. I sit watching this iguana in his glass tank trying to mate with a chameleon in the next tank.

SONIA. Can she cut hair?

ARTHUR. No, but the view is interesting. He keeps throwing himself against his glass tank and she keeps changing color. (*HE holds a bottle away from him to read the label.*) She's got a lot of style, Mrs. McNab. She's the only woman I know who's got a blue rinse and matching moustache.

(*SONIA comes behind him and puts her arms under his and begins to undo the top buttons of his shirt. HE continues to read the label.*)

SONIA. Don't unpack any more, Arthur. I'm rather tense and need relaxing. Can you unwind me? I can't undo this button.

ARTHUR. Because that's my belly button.

SONIA. Can we got to bed?

ARTHUR. I thought you'd never ask. I'll just open this '72 Batard Montrachet and take it in with us. It's quite cool enough.

SONIA. (*Begins to undress as SHE goes to the bedroom.*) I chilled it in my office.

ARTHUR. I'm glad to see you warmed up all the rest.

(*SHE gives an ambiguous groan.*)

ARTHUR. I'm sorry Norma was here. Very aggravating for you.

SONIA. I also had an irritating day at work. I arrived to find that Saatchi's had got an account we were pitching for ... then my secretary got hysterics because her boy friend phoned to say he wasn't leaving his wife.

ARTHUR. (*Opens wine.*) Those blokes with ginger hair never do.

SONIA. Then I was in the middle of a meeting with some clients, this Glaswegian bursts in and says "Where do you want your socket?" "Do you mind," I said. "I'm in a conference." "Room seventeen, I was told," he said.

ARTHUR. I'll put the blanket on. (*HE goes into the bedroom with the wine and two glasses.*)

SONIA. "Then you were told wrong," I said. "Mr. Hawkins said room seventeen," he said, "and it was urgent." (*Taking advantage of his absence SHE rummages in her bag and squirts something in her mouth.*) "But not today, sir." (*SHE coughs slightly.*) I was very respectful. Well, you know me—I always make a great effort to make working class people feel at their ease. (*SHE takes off her blouse.*) "Would you give Mr. Hawkins my compliments," I said, "And say I told him any day *next* week." Well, finally he left and we went back to discussing where we're going to shoot this commercial. They want it to look like a tropical beach in Barbados ... (*SHE goes through her bag again.*) ... and we've found this creek in the Isle of Dogs which is perfect—once we tart it up with some plastic trees. Then suddenly this great big Jamaican bursts in!

(*SHE is about to spray under her arms, but ARTHUR returns in an oriental dressing gown. This stops her.*)

ARTHUR. Just going to do myself a smoked salmon sandwich. (*HE goes behind the counter and quickly slices a generous helping.*) Full of protein. I need a bit of help these days. "I'm the foreman," he says.

SONIA. How did you know that?

ARTHUR. They always are.

SONIA. "I'm the foreman," he said, "and I was told to put a new plug in room seventeen on Friday." Out!

Out! I screamed. I do not want a new plug in my office
today!

ARTHUR. They leapt out in terror. You terrify me.
(*HE grates black pepper on the sandwich, then cuts
one of the lemons she has brought and squeezes it.*)

SONIA. But why should I be nicer to a black
electrician than I would be to a white one!

ARTHUR. Exactly! I'll just have a quick shower. (*HE
takes a bite of his sandwich as HE goes into the
bedroom.*)

SONIA. That is just another form of racial
discrimination.

ARTHUR. (*Off.*) That's right.

(*The sound of the SHOWER being turned on.*)

SONIA. I'm glad you agree.
ARTHUR. (*Off.*) I do.

(*Sound of SPLASHING and ARTHUR singing "Molly
     Malone."*
*SHE sprays herself with scent, makes one or two last
     minute checks, takes off her skirt then goes into
     the bathroom.*
A beat.
DOORBELL.
*SONIA comes out wrapping a negligee round
     herself.*)

SONIA. (*At bedroom door.*) Your doorbell.

ARTHUR. (*Off.*) If I answer it like this it'll take five
thousand off this apartment.

SONIA. I don't live here.

ARTHUR. (*Off.*) It's probably only Norma. Give her
an earful.

SONIA. Oh! Right! I'll enjoy that.

(*As we hear him resume singing, SHE closes the bedroom door and goes in a casual, flaunting way to the front door—opens it. HAROLD stands there not entirely sober.*)

HAROLD. I ... oh! Hello, Sonia. Of course. It's Friday.

SONIA. That's quite all right, Harold.. Do you want Arthur?

HAROLD. No. My Southern Comfort.

SONIA. Your what?

HAROLD. That bottle on the table. Would you mind? (*HE steps in. HE goes to the table and takes it. Stands there simmering and obviously not about to leave.*) Where is the double-crossing rat?

SONIA. Which rat are you referring to?

HAROLD. Arthur! The man whose life I saved in 1959 in St. Anton.

SONIA. I don't know about that.

HAROLD. That's how we first met. I was skiing in Austria and I stopped Arthur going over a two-hundred foot crevasse by throwing myself in his path. He got a bruise, I got a broken ankle, and what do I get thirty years later?

SONIA. Do I get a *little* clue, Harold?

HAROLD. I got my arse kicked! (*HE goes down to the kitchen and starts looking for a glass.*) *You* want a clue! No one ever gave me the slightest hint. (*HE pours himself a drink.*) Don't you think I should have been put in the picture a little earlier? Be fair Sonia. I travel five thousand miles through mosquito infested jungle, down rivers full of crocodiles, piranhas and poisonous water snakes. I get mugged in Lima, mugged in Bogota, get strip searched in New York, strip searched in London, cheated by the cab driver who brought me from Heathrow. I finally arrive home and my bags are packed! No surprise to anyone but me! Everyone has known for weeks that Norma was going to chuck me out, but me. You'd expect something a bit better than that from ... (*The drink and the emotion makes HIS voice tremble.*) ... your oldest friend. In wet weather my ankle still twinges. I let him break my ankle and he does this to me. (*Bursts into tears. SONIA goes to comfort him but stops herself.*) He could have tipped me the wink a bit earlier. Is that unreasonable, Sonia? (*HE blows his nose through her next line.*)

SONIA. (*A considering pause.*) No. Not at all, Harold. What did ... (*SHE eyes bedroom door.*) What did Norma actually say?

HAROLD. What she told you months ago. Apparently you were quite short with her. I don't blame you. You could hardly have enjoyed hearing that Norma was still madly in love with Arthur.

SONIA. (*A beat, then very calmly.*) Not really.

HAROLD. It couldn't have been fun for you, listening to her going on about how she couldn't get Arthur out of her system and it was giving her a nervous breakdown?

SONIA. No fun at all.

HAROLD. I'm glad you told her she was being pathetic.

SONIA. Oh, good.

HAROLD. In fact, the way you tore into her is the only redeeming factor in this entire squalid business. Just thinking about it in the pub. I was very pleased you told her she was making herself a laughing stock. I'm very touched by your support, Sonia.

SONIA. It was the least I could do.

(*While HE pours himself another drink SHE goes to the bedroom door and listens discreetly. Satisfied that ARTHUR is still singing in his shower, SHE makes her way back to Harold in a slow, speculative way.*)

SONIA. I can't remember all the details of the conversation ... (*SHE waits hoping for more information.*)

HAROLD. Well you must know better than I do. I just got it second-hand.

SONIA. I remember we discussed it for some time...

HAROLD. And I wasn't even included in the discussion. That's what hurts.

SONIA. I said something very similar.

HAROLD. Not that I blame Norma. She's always had this thing about Arthur and hates herself for it. Fair do's ... accepted and understood. What gets up my nose is flying half way round the world and when I get home ...

SONIA. You're out on the street!

HAROLD. And Arthur never even tipped me the wink of what was in the wind.

SONIA. Very naughty of him. I said to him months ago—you must tip Harold the wink. Give him a chance to prepare himself. Make other arrangements, etc.

HAROLD. You don't expect this sort of treatment from your oldest friend do you?

SONIA. You don't, Harold, but she's got him just where she wants him, so what can one do? (*Glances at the bedroom then decides to get rid of him.*) I'm very sorry it's worked out like this.

(*HE reaches for the Southern Comfort but SHE briskly screws on the stopper and puts the bottle in her Fortnum's carrier bag.*)

HAROLD. Everyone has known for weeks and Arthur didn't even give me the slightest clue.

SONIA. (*Briskly.*) People can be such a disappointment can't they? (*Hands him carrier.*) Got all your bits and pieces?

HAROLD. (*Blinking vaguely.*) Yes, I only came back for ...

SONIA. Oh, good! (*SHE opens the front door.*) I agree with you, Harold. He's let you down very badly over this.

HAROLD. (*Goes up to the door. The drink is telling.*) I'll be quite honest with you, Sonia. I think he's let me down very badly over this. (*HE exits carefully.*)

SONIA. (*Looks up and out for a moment.*) Mind the dustbins, Harold.

(*Sound of FALLING over a dustbin.*)

HAROLD. (*Off.*) Pardon?

SONIA. All the best, Harold. (*SHE shuts the door, glances at the bedroom malevolently and then considers her next step. SHE decides. Goes to the phone and dials. Calmly.*) Would you please give me a test ring on 381-5684? I'm not sure what difficulty I'm having. Thank you. (*SHE hangs up slowly to minimize the "ping" then goes to the bedroom door and opens it.*) Oh, darling! How sweet you look sitting up in bed waiting for me with two glasses of wine! I'll just put the lights out.

ARTHUR. (*Off.*) Was it Norma?

SONIA. No ... rather a pity. It was those Jehovah Witnesses. They never give up do they? (*SHE hums as SHE goes round turning off the lights.*)

ARTHUR. (*Off.*) I always say, I'm sorry, I'm Catholic!

SONIA. (*Laughs brightly.*) Oh, I say! That *is* funny! I wish I'd thought of that!

(*The room now lit only by the LIGHT from the bedroom. SHE enters the bedroom taking off her wrap. Door closes. A beat, then the PHONE rings. SONIA comes out doing up her wrap.*)

SONIA. (*Calling back.*) No, don't you bother, darling, I'll take it off the hook.

ARTHUR. (*Off.*) It might be my agent. See if it is, then take it off.

SONIA. All right, sweetheart.

ARTHUR. (*Off.*) If it's my bank manager pretend you're the answer phone like you did last week. That really foxed him.

SONIA. (*Into phone.*) Hello. (*Then sotto.*) Thank you. (*Presses the receiver cradle, coughs to drown the "ping," then releases it and speaks again into the phone.*) I'm sorry? Who is this? Dennis!! Oh, my God! It can't be you! (*Directs her voice to the bedroom and drops the phone.*) It's not you, Dennis ... Please say it's not you! (*SHE backs to the bedroom and leans weakly against the lintel.*)

ARTHUR. (*Appears at the bedroom door pulling up his trousers.*) What? Who? What's happening?

(*SONIA sinks slowly to the floor in a crumpled heap. ARTHUR feels his way to the nearest lamp. Stubs his toe. Turns on LIGHT.*

SONIA *points a shaking hand to the phone swinging on its lead. Her stark, croaking manner is an exotic cocktail of every Ibsen/Strindberg heroine.*)

SONIA. He's there. There!

ARTHUR. Who's there?

SONIA. My husband!

ARTHUR. (*HE instinctively steadies himself with his hands against the furniture letting his trousers drop slightly and then recovering them.*) Your husband!

SONIA. Hanging there!

ARTHUR. Hanging there! (*ARTHUR stares at the phone with matching, hypnotized horror, except his is genuine.*)

SONIA. He knows! He knows!

ARTHUR. (*Parched voice.*) He does? Knows what? (*HE does not move. Just stands there, keeping the tops of his trousers together.*)

SONIA. Oh, please, say it isn't you, Dennis.

(*ARTHUR looks from her to the phone.*)

SONIA. Please say it's not you.

(*ARTHUR looks to phone.*)

SONIA. It's a joke, isn't it? Some friend playing a practical joke! Yes?

ARTHUR. (*Nods in hopeful agreement towards the phone.*) Got to be. *Must* be a gag.

SONIA. Yes? (*SHE rises with both hands across her bosom.*) But it is you, isn't it, Dennis? (*SHE goes slowly to the phone.*) Oh my God! (*SHE picks up phone and speaks into it.*) Hullo, I'm sorry, Dennis. I dropped the phone. Such a shock. I see. How can I deny my affair with Arthur Vines?

ARTHUR. What?

SONIA. Your private detective has done a good job. Yes, Dennis, I've been having an affair for two years with Arthur Oscar Vines.

(*ARTHUR clutches his stomach as if in pain. HE doubles over.*)

SONIA. Yes. He is a commercial artist who specializes in book jackets. Yes, I've been coming to his flat, 29a Canfield Gardens, Fulham. Every Friday night. Yes, I lied to you about going to Monica's. Yes, his wife divorced him when she found me in the upstairs wardrobe. Your detective didn't know about the wardrobe? I'm glad there's something he doesn't know.

ARTHUR. It's not happening!

SONIA. Yes, Dennis, I have lied to you for years.

ARTHUR. Why me?

SONIA. Yes, every time I told you I was going to help Monica in her restaurant in Sevenoaks, I spent the night with Arthur. Yes, I do love him, and I would like to share the rest of my life with him—not just one day a week!

ARTHUR. What are you saying? Just one night a week is wonderful! That's all I ever wanted. (*HE runs back into the bedroom.*)

SONIA. (*Directs her voice in that direction.*) How does he feel? Well, he's not sure what he feels about anything, unless he asks Norma first. The future? Well I had hoped to get him to move out. Get away from this hag's influence. He would have asked me to live

with him a long time ago if it wasn't for Madam Svengali
upstairs.

ARTHUR. No, Sonia. Just one day a week! That's
all I ever wanted.

SONIA. You're coming over here?

ARTHUR. No! No!

SONIA. I'll come home then, collect a few things
and move into a hotel.

ARTHUR. (*Abandons putting on the other sock.*)
That's an idea ... yes. Not wonderful but it'll do. (*HE
runs round putting on more lights and gathering up
her clothes.*)

SONIA. If you kill Arthur, that won't make me love
you any better, Dennis. Yes, Arthur is here. Would
you like to speak to him?

ARTHUR. (*Backing.*) I'yer ... I' yer...

SONIA. I see. Well, he doesn't want to speak to
you either, Dennis. I'll come home now. (*SHE hangs
up.*)

ARTHUR. I never wanted you to leave him, Sonia!

(*During the following HE frantically helps HER to
dress.*)

SONIA. Crafty old bugger has had a detective
following me for the past three months!

ARTHUR. When did I ever ask you to leave him? I
never wanted to break up your marriage! I would
never have asked you to leave him, Sonia.

(*As SHE buttons up her blouse, HE kneels to put on
her shoes.*)

ARTHUR. Just one night a week was perfect!
Every Friday night and our occasional weekends in

Amsterdam! You've said yourself we had the sort of relationship you've been trying to find for years. Passionately committed to each other, but only for one night a week!

SONIA. I had some Tibetan earrings. You spineless little runt.

ARTHUR. Little runt? It's not my fault your husband has found out.

SONIA. (*Screams.*) My Tibetan earrings!

ARTHUR. Tibetan earrings!? (*Searches.*) What's this? (*Holds up a red bunch of something on a chain.*) No, that's a bunch of paper clips. I never wanted you to leave him. All this fantastic food and booze you bring every Friday. I never wanted to change a thing! What do Tibetan earrings look like?

SONIA. I remember now. I didn't wear them because they clashed with my Afghan bracelet. Where's that?

ARTHUR. Afghan bracelet? (*Searches.*) She wants an Afghan bracelet now. When I woke up this morning, the sun was streaming into my bedroom. I leapt out of bed and rowed ten miles—on my rowing machine. I went into the bathroom and looked at myself and said yes, Arthur ... the doctor is right! You do have the body of a young man of 24. Apart from a few laughter lines, a little thinning of the hair and the fact that I once was in love with Susan Haywood. I felt so good this morning. I might have known it wouldn't last. I wish I hadn't woken up this morning. Wish I'd slept right through today. This Afghan ...?

SONIA. Six ropes of jet with a large orange shell in the middle. You weak-kneed stupid blob of jelly.

ARTHUR. Me stupid?! Why didn't *you* notice a man following you for the past three months? Was Dennis *very* angry?

SONIA. (*Puts on jacket and makes up.*) Very polite. He said, very reasonably, that he knew all about us, but there was a terrible cold charm in his voice which I've only heard once before—when he sacked three thousand chemical workers at the Gateshead factory. They wanted extra money for something. We were dining at home. The phone went. He listened for a moment then said, "Make them all redundant." He then calmly finished his Dover sole.

ARTHUR. Dover sole? We had one last month.

SONIA. He was like that just now. Very charming and quite, quite terrifying.

ARTHUR. (*Fast losing his nerve as HE sorts through the junk.*) But I never asked you to live with me, Sonia. (*Finds an object which roughly matches the description.*) Here's your Afghan bracelet. No, it's my Kawasaki distributor cap.

SONIA. There's going to be murder when I get home. Murder! (*SHE goes to the front door.*)

ARTHUR. Suppose he turns up here? What do I say? What's my attitude? What steps do I take? Apart from long ones, that is.

SONIA. How I despise you. One shot across your bow and you quake. Now wonder Norma treats you with such contempt.

ARTHUR. Norma has nothing to do with this. What can I do?

SONIA. (*As SHE exits.*) I'll keep you posted.

ARTHUR. Advise me! You've dropped me in it! (*HE shouts up the area steps with outstretched, imploring arms.*) What are you doing to me, Sonia? (*A dustbin lid comes HURTLING down just missing his head. HE leaps adroitly inside then peers out.*) Please, Sonia ... not the actual bin. They don't come till next Thursday. (*A load of garbage falls on him. He hastily darts within.*

Shuts door. A beat then the bin itself is thrown down
the stone steps.)

(*Slight pause. A dog BARKS.*)

ARTHUR. What's happening, Arthur? (*Pause.
Then the ebullient notes of MOZART'S HORN
CONCERTO is heard from above. HE goes to the
phone and dials. Into phone.*) Would you please
come down a moment, Norma? Yes ... now. This is
more important than your workout. (*HE hangs ups.
Stares ahead then goes to the middle door and
makes a passage through the junk. MUSIC stops.*) I
must have a drink. Where's my Southern Comfort?
That's what I need now. A bit of Southern Comfort.
(*Searches.*) It was here a minute ago!

(*Middle door opens and NORMA appears in a red
leotard and short practice skirt—a kind of ice
skater's kit.*)

NORMA. Is it my Mozart? I turned it down low.
(*Glances round a little anxiously.*) You sure you want
to see me? I don't want to upset Sonia. There's some
cauliflower on your shoulder. (*Removes it.*) Where is
Sonia?
ARTHUR. Gone.
NORMA. Gone? Oh, dear! (*Then, not entirely
displeased.*) Did I upset her that much?
ARTHUR. Her husband phoned. He's found out
we've been having an affair for two years.
NORMA. Oooooooooh! I say! I thought you looked
a little peaky!
ARTHUR. He knows everything! Where the hell is
my Southern Comfort? (*Searches.*)

NORMA. How did he find out?

ARTHUR. He's had a private detective onto her for the past three months.

NORMA. And Sonia never suspected?

ARTHUR. No.

NORMA. But she's always been so careful about him not finding out. Once she thought one of her husband's executives lived nearby and she used to come in a grey wig.

ARTHUR. (*Distractedly searching.*) Grey wig?

NORMA. Looked as if she'd made it out of Brillo pads. Then there's this subterfuge about her helping in her friend's restaurant. She always phones Monica to ask the dish of the day, so she can tell Dennis when she goes home Saturday morning. She's carried on as if she was having an affair Mr. Gorbachev. I'm astonished he even suspected her!

ARTHUR. And the moment he said he's caught her she said she's going to leave him for me!

(*NORMA gives a smothered guffaw.*)

ARTHUR. You may think this ludicrous, but this is the moment, that Sonia, in her heart of hearts, has been yearning for.

NORMA. To come and live with you?

ARTHUR. You find that laughable?

NORMA. Darling, you've always had a certain appeal for neurotic, unstable women—like myself, for instance—but even Sonia isn't daft enough to leave a Queen Anne house and two Canelletoes for this damp basement and your British Rail posters.

ARTHUR. Sonia loves me, Norma. You don't know what the word means, but Sonia does love me!

(*This suddenly goes home. NORMA's mouth tightens. ARTHUR, unaware, as HE now searches through assorted bottles in the cupboards, etc.*)

ARTHUR. I know Dennis is a millionaire captain of industry. Appears on TV talk shows to discuss the state of the nation. I know he's already got a CBE and she could be Lady Bradshaw any moment, but she does love me!

(*As HER tears spurt, SHE turns away and, taking off her towelling sweat band from her hair, dabs her eyes.*)

ARTHUR. She would give up all those wonderful charge accounts, her gold Barclay card ... platinum American Express card and white Porsche for me! She'd even take her son from Harrow! He's got to cost ten grand a year not counting his grass!

(*NORMA turns and looks out of the French windows. SHE takes some deep breaths to collect herself.*)

ARTHUR. And next term he's going to start oboe lessons! Well, we all know what that can lead to. We had all that with Juliet's bassoon lessons. That cost us £500 years ago. Not that I begrudged it. Her playing gave me much pleasure.

NORMA. Actually it cost us £750 and all she could play was "Half a Pound of Tuppenny Rice." We worked it out. It cost us £28 a note. (*She is back to her old form.*)

ARTHUR. Juliet played the solo part in "Pop Goes the Weasel" at the School Girls' Festival of Music at

Ludlow. Why are you always knocking her? (*HE goes into the bedroom.*)

NORMA. She criticizes me often enough. I took her out to lunch this afternoon and while I was pouring my heart out to her she said I had finally convinced her there isn't life after marriage.

ARTHUR. (*Returns with wine.*) Norma, I know I'm asking a big favor, but could you stop thinking about yourself for two minutes?

NORMA. Certainly.

ARTHUR. What can I do?

NORMA. She's gone home?

ARTHUR. To pack a case and move into a hotel. Just one day a week is all I ever wanted from Sonia.

NORMA. Tell *him* that.

ARTHUR. Tell *him*?

NORMA. He can't know that and Sonia isn't going to tell him. It's something he will be pleased to hear. He loves her, doesn't he?

ARTHUR. Mad about her.

NORMA. He might be cross with her now, but he is twenty years older. He knows it'll be in his best interests to forgive her eventually.

ARTHUR. You could be right!

NORMA. So phone him.

ARTHUR. Phone him?

NORMA. And say you only ever wanted Sonia for one day a week. You can't stand her more than one day a week. That will give him a trump card to play. He'll be very grateful to you.

ARTHUR. Your degree in psychology is bringing me dividends at last.

NORMA. Say that as far as you're concerned Sonia has never been anything more to you than a Friday night amusement.

ARTHUR. That's right! (*HE moves excitedly round the room.*)

NORMA. So phone him now.

ARTHUR. (*Stops.*) Now?

NORMA. Get the boot in before Sonia gets home.

ARTHUR. Absolutely!

NORMA. Simply say—very casually—that Sonia and you are strictly a one-day-a-week event.

ARTHUR. I like it.

NORMA. Say you'll pop over and tell him face to face you never wanted to come between them.

ARTHUR. Think I should phone now?

NORMA. He's in the book, isn't he? (*NORMA thumbs through one of the phone books.*)

ARTHUR. Dunno. I've always phoned her at her office. (*Hands her spectacles.*)

NORMA. Remember, you will be telling him something he will be pleased to hear. You've got everything to gain by phoning him and nothing to lose!

ARTHUR. There's no argument.

NORMA. She didn't think twice about admitting her affair. She blew the whistle on you immediately!

ARTHUR. Didn't hesitate!

NORMA. And you're an innocent party.

ARTHUR. I am. That is exactly my situation!

NORMA. (*Reads.*) Ah! Dennis Bradshaw C.B.E., Cheyne Walk, SW3 This is him all right! (*SHE writes on the pad, tears it off and hands it to him, then hands him back his glasses.*)

ARTHUR. Terrific! (*Dials.*) All the sevens ... one two one three. I'll get in first with my version.

NORMA. You've got a trump card you can put right into his hand.

ARTHUR. No question about it. (*HE hangs up abruptly.*) I just need a little drink first.

NORMA. There's some of his wine here.

ARTHUR. No, I need a drop of Southern Comfort. (*Searches.*) I must have put it somewhere safe.

ARTHUR. (*Dials number.*) It was sheer blackmail for Sonia to say she was leaving him for you.

ARTHUR. If I phoned later it'll be the cheap rate.

NORMA. Sonia will be furious with you but she'll come round in six months and you can carry on as before. (*SHE listens at the phone for a moment then hands it to Arthur.*)

ARTHUR. (*Into phone.*) Hello? Oh, good evening. Is that Dennis Bradshaw? My name is Arthur Vines. You don't know me personally but you know that I have been your wife's lover every Friday for the past two years at 29a Canfield Gardens, Fulham. Now I'm just ringing to say ...

(*During the above NORMA has got her head close to his to listen to the phone.*)

NORMA. (*Hand over mouthpiece.*) Glass of wine and a chat. (*Removes her hand.*)

ARTHUR. (*Into phone.*) I wondered if we could meet—for a glass of wine ... and a chat. Just that er ... me and Sonia ... we're strictly Friday nights only. (*Surprised.*) Well, yes ... by all means. You know where I live? Yes, of course you do. Er ... yes ... I'll look forward to seeing you, Mr. Bradshaw. Oh, right. Er ... cheerio then, Dennis. (*He hangs up.*)

(*THEY both stare at each other blankly.*)

NORMA. He said he was delighted to hear from you.

ARTHUR. Has he gone off his head?

NORMA. He said he was thrilled you had phoned to ask him over! What can that mean?

ARTHUR. It means he's going to arrive with a blunt instrument. He was very angry when he phoned up. Twenty minutes later, he's thrilled to talk to me. I don't think we should have invited him round Norma. In fact, on reflection, I don't think we should have phoned him at all! Can you go insane in twenty minutes?

NORMA. My Uncle Stanley did. Ten minutes after preaching a sermon on Sodom and Gomorrah he cycled down Abergavenny High Street wearing nothing but his dog collar. He was very charming to the police when they caught him in the Brecon Beacons.

(*There is a CLUNK as someone is heard tripping over the dustbin lid in the area.*)

ARTHUR. (*Instinctively clutches Norma.*) Has he come by rocket?

(*The front door opens and SONIA enters. THEY separate at once.*)

SONIA. Ah, Norma! Thought you'd be here. In times of stress he flies back to Mummy doesn't he? I was very peeved when I learned you had got Arthur to tell Harold to go because you couldn't get Arthur out of your system. I was furious with you, Arthur, for agreeing to do it. (*To Norma.*) Next time you want Arthur to get rid of your unwanted lovers, you will ask me first! O.K.?

NORMA. O.K.

SONIA. Because next time I won't just get the operator to give me a test ring and pretend it was Dennis ... next time it really will be Dennis. He'll chuck me out and I shall have to move in with you, Arthur. You'll have me seven days a week and that wouldn't suit you at all, would it, darling?

(*ARTHUR gives her a distant look. HE turns away and stares. Bangs his head to clear it. HE turns back to her and opens his mouth to speak but he doesn't for a moment.*)

ARTHUR. A test ring?

SONIA. (*Giggles.*) When Harold came back for his Southern Comfort and told me how you'd got rid of him, (*SHE goes to kitchen and cuts herself some salami.*) for a ludicrous couple of seconds, I even believed it myself. It gave me a very nasty turn. I'm delighted I've done the same for you! (*SHE takes a bite of salami.*)

ARTHUR. (*Politely.*) It wasn't your husband who rang?

SONIA. The telephone operator.

ARTHUR. You were talking to a telephone operator?

SONIA. Only to start—most of the time I was talking to the dialling tone. (*To Norma.*) If you ever manipulate Arthur again—next time there'll be *real* trouble.

NORMA. I'm sorry.

SONIA. O.K. Let's forget it. Good night, Norma.

(*NORMA doesn't move. Just looks at Arthur then back to Sonia.*)

ARTHUR. A test ring?

SONIA. (*Going up to middle door.*) Yes—while you were having a shower. I asked the operator to test the line. (*Removes a cabin trunk and opens the middle door wide.*) Good night, Norma.

ARTHUR. Will you tell me why I ever listen to you Norma?

NORMA. You said her husband had phoned!

ARTHUR. How did you come to persuade me to phone her husband?

SONIA. Pardon?

ARTHUR. I would never, ever, have phoned Dennis if you hadn't suggested it.

SONIA. I'm sorry?

ARTHUR. (*Turns to Sonia.*) You may have pretended to speak to your husband, Sonia, but after you left I didn't pretend. I phoned him and admitted everything ... according to Norma' s instructions.

NORMA. (*Increasingly nervous.*) Not instructions— I just casually suggested ...

ARTHUR. Norma said there was no point in denying anything now that Dennis had found out.

SONIA. (*Starkly.*) You admitted every Friday night for the past two years?

ARTHUR. Then invited him over for a drink. Just to tell him you were no more than my Friday night friend.

SONIA. (*Delicate and faint.*) I wish you hadn't done that.

ARTHUR. I think I'll pop off for a few days. You ladies can entertain him when he arrives. Give him a glass of his own wine and cut him a slice of his smoked salmon. (*Looks at his watch.*) Yes ... I think my continued presence here will just confuse the issue. I'll just toss a few things into a bag. (*HE goes into the bedroom.*)

SONIA. You told him to phone Dennis?

NORMA. I just ... sort of ... in a way ... well, how can I put it? Yes.

SONIA. (*Matter of fact.*) You have wrecked my marriage and destroyed my relationship with Arthur. (*Closes the middle door and comes slowly to Norma.*)

NORMA. I just thought ...

(*ARTHUR comes out stuffing clothes into a grip then stuffs some of his laundry into the bag.*
NORMA moves so that Arthur is between them.)

NORMA. ... it is only fair that Arthur should be given the chance to present his side of it. Naturally, I would not have advised that ...

(*SONIA comes round Arthur. NORMA "casually" moves in front of Arthur and edges up to the middle door.*)

NORMA. ... had I known you were only talking to a test ring.

SONIA. (*Moves up to the middle door and blocks it with the cabin trunk.*) But you told Arthur to phone *my* husband?

(*ARTHUR ignores them as HE goes round collecting items of clothing, papers, books, etc.*
The TWO WOMEN are oblivious of him as THEY stare at each other—SONIA with an implacable incredulity and NORMA with alert defensiveness.)

NORMA. Your hysterical behavior placed us in such a position ... (*Begins to rally.*) Arthur had to defend himself.

ARTHUR. No Arthur ... it's time you faced up to what you are—a stupid old wanker.

(*NORMA edges discreetly to the front door.*
SONIA hurls the dress-makers dummy at the front door thus blocking Norma's second potential exit.)

SONIA. Oooooooooh! (*Then a great screech.*) You evil old *BAG!*

(*NORMA gets behind Arthur but HE passes between them with his grip.*)

ARTHUR. You always were ... always will be.
NORMA. Well, quite honestly, Sonia. (*Gives a wavering look at the bedroom.*) ... I don't really want to enter into any vulgar debate.
SONIA. Vulgar debate! (*SHE grabs the top of Norma's elasticated leotard.*)

(*ARTHUR takes his passport out of a drawer and flicks through it.*
NORMA takes a pace back. SONIA still holds it. NORMA takes another pace. SONIA lets the leotard go.)

NORMA. I hope that makes you feel better.
ARTHUR. At least my passport isn't out of date so I can leave the country.
NORMA. I shall go now. I have no wish to descend to physical violence. I'm sure that's how you used to settle things in Bermondsey—before you acquired your posh accent—but it doesn't really suit me!

(*SONIA hits her with her bag.*)

NORMA. Oh really, Sonia—what a ridiculous nouveau riche woman you are! I've always said you're just kid gloves and no drawers!

(*As NORMA goes towards French windows, SHE pinches Sonia.*
SONIA cuts off her exit and gives her a swinging blow to the stomach with her bag. NORMA is knocked back in a sprawling heap on the sofa. SHE is up immediately. BOTH eye each other as NORMA adjusts her clothes. BOTH are slightly breathless.
ARTHUR takes some files from a filing cabinet and puts them in his grip.)

ARTHUR. But that's the story of your life, Arthur. You've always allowed people to take advantage of you.

(*NORMA goes calmly to Sonia and rips off the bow from Sonia's blouse then stands back and rips the blouse lapel.*)

ARTHUR. That's why you've now got a face like a rumpled pillow. It bears the impression of the last person who sat on you.

(*SONIA makes a threatening move.*
NORMA runs into the kitchen and closes the flap.)

ARTHUR. Once you admit your deficiencies, life will be much happier for you.
SONIA. (*Looks 'round then goes up to the middle door, picks up the épée and, flexing it, goes to the*

kitchen.) You're now going to get this across your arse, Norma.

(*NORMA leaps on the stool then onto the kitchen counter as SONIA lifts up the flap.*
NORMA turns away to bend to pick up something. SONIA goes to whack her across the buttocks, but NORMA spins around clutching the eighteen inch salami and knocks the épée out of Sonia's hand.
NORMA scrambles off the counter and runs to the French windows, but SONIA leaps and grabs the back of Norma's leotard at the top.
NORMA gives her a backward wallop with the salami which winds SONIA and makes her release her hold.
As NORMA unlocks the French windows, SONIA recovers. SHE runs to Norma as NORMA runs out into the garden. SONIA follows her out.)

ARTHUR. (*Zipping up his grip.*) No, quite frankly, old boy, you're in the shit and you've only got yourself to blame.

(*During this there are a series of strangulated YELPS heard off in the garden, then SONIA backs in through the French windows dragging Norma by the back of her leotard.*
NORMA out-stretches her arms against the lintel. This holds her.
SONIA continues to back and the elastic material stretches out behind Norma like a great red bat's wing.
BOTH WOMEN strain. There is a still impasse like a pause in samurai.)

ARTHUR. Instant flight. That's the only thing left for you. Sonny Jim.

(*HE collects a bottle of the wine from the kitchen counter. NORMA suddenly backs against SONIA, who topples back onto the sofa with NORMA on top of her.*)

ARTHUR. Instant flight!

(*HE puts the bottle in his grip and zips it up. NORMA suddenly leaps forward. SONIA holds on. The leotard comes slowly apart at the seams. NORMA holds the front. SONIA still holds the back. The leotard rips slowly.*)

NORMA. (*Between gritted teeth.*) Bitch!
SONIA. (*Ditto.*) Whore!
ARTHUR. (*Collects his mac, kicks aside the dummy, and exits through the front door. On exiting.*) No wonder they didn't make you a Lance Corporal.

(*The only connection between the women now is that part of the leotard that runs between the top of Norma's legs.*
Both strain with NORMA holding the front part at chest height. There is a final rip. NORMA is propelled to the French windows holding only the front part, leaving SONIA lurching back holding the back part.
As NORMA leaps out of the French windows, SONIA runs after her, grabbing up a bottle. Screams and the CRASH of a bottle breaking are heard off.)

CURTAIN

ACT II

An hour later. Darkness, but for a spill of LIGHT from a STREET LAMP above.

A DARK SHAPE passes in the area. Front door opens quietly, a FIGURE enters.

The door closes.

The FIGURE moves down to the kitchen. A kitchen SPOTLIGHT goes on and we see it is NORMA. SHE wears an elegant cocktail dress and has arranged her hair as if for a film premiere. SHE carries a tray of cocktail snacks.

SHE puts the tray down and turns on a TABLE LIGHT. The room is as disorderly as before except that now the curtain over the middle door has been drawn.

SHE closes the French windows and tidies the sofa cushions. SHE then gets an air freshener from the cupboard and sprays the room briefly. SHE stands the dress-making dummy upright and replaces the fencing mask on top.

SHE then picks up the coil of rope and pulls aside the middle door curtain, revealing ARTHUR sitting cross-legged in Yoga style on one of the packing cases with his eyes shut.

SHE screams and HE leaps with fright.

NORMA. Arthur! Why do you do these things to me?

ARTHUR. Why do you do these thing to *me?* I was in a deep trance mediating on my Yin and Yang, and now my heart is going like a steam hammer!

NORMA. Why were you in the dark?

ARTHUR. I didn't want you to know I was back. I intend to deal with Dennis on my own—just the two of us, face to face. The final showdown.

NORMA. But I've got myself all ready. I've made some cocktail snacks. I caused all this trouble. The least I can do is stand by you.

ARTHUR. The best you can do for me, Norma is to go back upstairs and stay there.

NORMA. But I've got myself all dolled up!

ARTHUR. Well, you can just un-doll yourself.

NORMA. I'll tidy up first. We don't want Dennis to think you live in a slum.

NORMA. Why don't you change your trousers and make yourself look nice? (*SHE shakes out a polar bearskin rug and lays it on the floor.*) I'm so glad you came back.

ARTHUR. I very nearly didn't.

NORMA. Where did you go to?

ARTHUR. I was on my way to Malaga to make a new life for myself.

NORMA. Oh, yes. Your nephew, Jack, has always said he'd give you a job there, washing up in his hotel.

ARTHUR. He told *me* I'd be banqueting manager. Anyway, I was well on my way to Spain, but I decided to turn back.

NORMA. How far did you get?

ARTHUR.Safeways in the High Street. What happened to Sonia?

NORMA. Don't know. She chased me up the alley.

ARTHUR. She didn't catch you?

NORMA. Very nearly got me in Jubilee Terrace, but I dodged down the passage behind Woolworth's, leapt over Mr. Dobson's fence and hid behind his potting shed.

ARTHUR. Obviously your floppy legs have made a total recovery.

NORMA. I'm very sorry about this.

ARTHUR. You only did what you thought was best.

NORMA. (*A beat.*) Anyway, when Dennis arrives, I'm sure it won't be as bad as you think. I'm sure a punch on the nose will be maximum. Why did you come back, Arthur? Was it because you didn't want me to have to deal with Dennis on my own?

ARTHUR. I came back because I've got the VAT people coming on Monday, I having my wisdom tooth out on Tuesday, the Inland Revenue want to see me Wednesday and the doctor wants to see my piles on Thursday. In fact, when I thought of my *routine* appointments for next week, seeing Dennis tonight doesn't seem half so bad.

NORMA. Just an unpleasant five minutes or so.

ARTHUR. And stand by with a bunch of cold keys.

(*ARTHUR goes to his desk, turns on the LIGHT and begins to draw.*)

NORMA. You're going to work now?

ARTHUR. Why not? It might be my last book jacket. Anyway, I owe Mr. Spurdle at the art shop £465 for materials. He phoned me this morning and said he wouldn't give me another inch of charcoal till I paid him two hundred on account. I said, Mr. Spurdle, how can I owe you £465 for charcoal? If you supplied me with all the charcoal you'd get by burning down the New Forest it wouldn't amount to £465. Dennis won't send the boys round, will he?

NORMA. What boys?

ARTHUR. A couple of yuppies on his staff who'd think it fun to blow off my knee caps.

NORMA. When he arrives we'll just play it by ear.

ARTHUR. You're right. And by the end of the evening I might only have one ear to play with. He might do a Van Gogh on me.

NORMA. This is interesting? What's this? (*SHE holds up an old horse's harness made of leather straps, chain and brass rings.*)

ARTHUR. A horse's harness I borrowed from the pub. I must return it.

NORMA. What was that book?

ARTHUR. A biography called *An East Anglican Boyhood.* I drew a horse and cart and a boy.

NORMA. How does it go? I can't work out these traps.

ARTHUR. (*Crossing to her.*) It goes with the collar. (*Produces horse collar from alcove and stands it on sideboard. Then gets a fat kit bag from the alcove and places it behind the collar.*)

NORMA. What was that kit bag for?

ARTHUR. A paperback edition of *The Soldier's Return.* The harness goes over the horse like this, you see? (*HE arranges the harness over the kit bag, linking up with the collar.*) The shafts to through these holes here ...

NORMA. You couldn't get a horse down here?

ARTHUR. No, I copied the horse from Stubbs. (*HE goes to his shelves and gets down an art book.*) He didn't do many cart horses, but there's a wonderful one here I copied ... (*HE shows her.*)

NORMA. Ah!

ARTHUR. And this is my version. (*HE gets a book.*)

NORMA. That's beautiful, Arthur.

ARTHUR. (*Genuinely pleased.*) You really like it?

NORMA. It's enchanting.

ARTHUR. You're not just saying that?

NORMA. No! If I saw that in a bookshop, I'd know that this was the story of a 1930's childhood. A pastoral idyll about Suffolk in, say, 1934.

ARTHUR. I was trying for 1934.

NORMA. You've caught the period perfectly.

ARTHUR. Thanks. Sonia said it looked a bit dated.

NORMA. It was supposed to be!

ARTHUR. I know. She's good in bed, but you won't find an ounce of romance in Sonia.

NORMA. And she's got a few ounces to choose from. I didn't mean that. I could cut my tongue out. What's that gurgling sound?

ARTHUR. My stomach. Thinking of Sonia reminds me of Dennis.

NORMA. Shall I go or stay?

ARTHUR. Perhaps you could hang around for a bit.

NORMA. As a third party I might be able to present your point of view better than you can.

ARTHUR. Yes.

NORMA. I'll make it very clear to him that you only ever wanted Sonia for one night a week. That should please him.

ARTHUR. Of course, there is a possibility that he might not be too ecstatic even about one night a week!

NORMA. I shall make it clear that you never wanted a deeper relationship.

ARTHUR. I still can't work out why he was so charming to me on the phone.

NORMA. I'm sure he'd consider it very bad form to lose his temper. He always seems the perfect gentleman on TV.

ARTHUR. You'll be pleasant to him?

NORMA. I intend to be *extremely* charming. Why do you think I'm in this kit? I owe it to you, Arthur. (*Rises and resumes tidying.*) When Dennis arrives I shall be the perfect hostess.

ARTHUR. I will say how sorry I am to have caused him distress and will do anything I can to make amends. If he wants to knock my teeth down my throat, I shall say—"There they are, Dennis!" (*HE does a great grin.*) Help yourself.

NORMA. I should take them out first.

ARTHUR. Perhaps we should have a little music playing softly in the background. (*HE goes through his cassettes and puts one on and resumes his work. The Valkyrie (Act III) blares out.*)

NORMA. (*SHE turns it off.*) I don't think "Ride of the Valkyries" is quite right. Haven't you got any Mantovani?

ARTHUR. I don't like Mantovani.

NORMA. He does.

ARTHUR. How do you know?

NORMA. I heard him once on *Desert Island Discs.* When he's shipwrecked he wants to listen to Mantovani, while he reads *Tess of the D'Urbervilles.* You need the sort of music you don't listen to.

ARTHUR. There's a scratched 78 of Mel Torme singing "Blue Moon."

NORMA. Oh, darling! Have you still got that? (*SHE is quite moved.*) I gave you that for your 21st.

ARTHUR. We don't need music. (*Returns to his desk.*) I'm feeling very relaxed about everything now. I've never been more at peace with myself.

(*The DOORBELL rings. HE leaps with fright, knocking over his pit of pencils and brushes.*)

ARTHUR. Oh, God, Norma! I'm not made for this life!

(*While HE scrambles about picking them up, NORMA takes a lipstick out of her evening bag and applies it. SHE then runs to the easy chair, picks up a magazine and arranges herself decorously.*
ARTHUR sidles up to the window blind and discreetly pulls the cord so that he can peep out through a slit. As HE bends the entire blind flies up revealing HAROLD outside.
HE smiles at Norma and waves his bottle of Southern Comfort at her.)

NORMA. Oh, God! Not him again!

(*ARTHUR opens the door.*)

HAROLD. Yes. It's me again! I can lip read. You didn't know that, did you, Norma? I picked it up because I make a lot of wax.
NORMA. I didn't know that either.
HAROLD. Oh, yes. I have to get them syringed a lot.
ARTHUR. This is not really a very convenient time, Harold ...
HAROLD. (*From his position, framed in the doorway, HE takes a single, very careful stride into the room.*) It baffles medical science, you know? Oh, yes. (*It is now apparent that HE has had more than a few.*) Doctors don't know why some people are big wax makers and some people are little wax makers.
ARTHUR. How can I help you, Harold? Why have you come back?

HAROLD. Why? (*HE glances for a moment, then the bottle reminds him.*) Oh, yes. I was on my way to Billericay ... thinking about things. ... and I suddenly felt very bad about this, Arthur. This is your Southern Comfort—not mine. I brought it back as a gift for you. It's all yours so take it. (*HE offers the bottle which now contains an inch of whiskey.*)

ARTHUR. Thank you very much, Harold. Very kind of you.

HAROLD. Extremely small- minded of me to take it back. Forgive me. (*Enters the room and makes his way to the kitchen.*) I feel very bad about it. (*Puts the bottle on the counter and gets a glass.*

ARTHUR. You were provoked.

HAROLD. (*Empties the bottle into a glass and takes a sip.*) I thought so—at the time, but all this business about me and Norma ... this trouble she's been having ... all my fault. *I've* done it to her. I'm the cause of her floppy bust.

NORMA. Legs actually, Harold.

HAROLD. Fact is, Norma, somewhere along the line ... (*Lurches over to her.*) I lost a little of my magic for you. (*Sits on the arm of the easy chair and puts his hand round her shoulder.*) That's what you were trying to tell me, wasn't it?

NORMA. Why don't you ring me tomorrow, Harold?

HAROLD. So be it! (*Rises.*) I'll take the high road. I only popped back to return Arthur's whiskey and to collect the last of my chattels. (*HE finishes the whiskey.*) I won't bother you again. (*HE crosses over and gets his foot stuck in the polar bear's mouth. HE stares down at it.*) I'm not going back to Hermione, by the way.

NORMA. Really?

HAROLD. (*Shakes his foot.*) No, I've got a room in Dollis Hill.

NORMA. How enterprising of you!

(*ARTHUR disengages Harold's foot.*)

HAROLD. That bear has played hell with my toe-caps. Robin was driving me to Hermione and I suddenly thought there might be going a room in his house.

NORMA. And was there going a room?

HAROLD. Yes. A nice room. Suit me till I get myself organized. He had a pair of sexy black knickers hanging up behind the door, left there by some tart, he said.

NORMA. How amusing!

(*There is something about her tone that makes ARTHUR look at her sharply.*)

HAROLD. He's a lad! Had all the girls in the office.

NORMA. (*Slightly tight-lipped.*) Is that so?

HAROLD. I've left my Zulu war dance outfit upstairs.

NORMA. Those dusty things in the box room?

HAROLD. I brought them in a canoe all the way up the Zambezi.

NORMA. I'll go up and get them. (*Rises and goes to the middle door.*) And isn't there a big hollowed out log somewhere?

HAROLD. That's the war drum. You made me put it in the garden shed.

NORMA. It weighs a ton. Be careful of your bad back.

(*ROBIN appears at the area window .*)

ARTHUR. (*Going to the door.*) This won't take long, will it, Harold?

HAROLD. You don't mind if Robin comes through to collect my gear, do you?

ARTHUR. (*Opening door.*) I've got rather a full diary this evening.

ROBIN. (*Enters.*) Hello again!

ARTHUR. Hello. The garden shed is out there! (*HE opens the French windows.*)

ROBIN. Thank you, Mr. Vines. (*Passing Norma.*) Good evening, Mrs. Vines.

NORMA. Good evening, Mr. Toovey.

ROBIN. Excuse me. (*Exits into the garden.*)

NORMA. So it's just those sharp sticks and that feathery thing, is it, Harold?

HAROLD. The hunting spears and the headdress plumes ... yes, please, Norma.

NORMA. I'll give them a dust. (*Exits through the middle door.*)

HAROLD. You look a bit unhappy.

ARTHUR. I'm not feeling too jolly.

HAROLD. I'm very touched you should feel unhappy about me. More than touched, moved ... (*Goes to Arthur.*) You do believe that, Arthur? I'm really moved.

ARTHUR. I do, Harold.

HAROLD. (*Embraces Arthur.*) I'm really moved, Arthur. (*Gives a muffled sob into Arthur's neck.*) I know you tried to help me. You did your best. You failed, but don't be sad about it.

(*During this ARTHUR has been looking over Harold's shoulder, hoping that no one enters.*)

HAROLD. No need. Things are going to work out.

ARTHUR. I'm pleased to hear it.

HAROLD. I've had time to reflect. Norma only *thinks* she can't get you out of her cistern.

ARTHUR. System.

HAROLD. It's nothing more an everyday female complaint. Nothing more than menoperusal insecurity.

ARTHUR. You could be right.

HAROLD. I know I'm right. Affects a lot of women ...

ARTHUR. The menoperusal.

HAROLD. That's right. They get these chemical changes in their body.and it's these harmonial changes in their body making them a little unbalanced.

ARTHUR. You don't say?

HAROLD. I do say! I definitely do say!

HAROLD. There's nothing seriously wrong with me and Norma, it's just her harmonia playing her up. You might like to tell her later.

ARTHUR. I will. I'll tell her to stop playing with her harmonia.

HAROLD. (*A moment of sudden sobriety.*) You making fun of me?

ARTHUR. (*Hastily.*) Not at all, Harold. Just that I've got a few problems.

HAROLD. I won't intrude further.

ARTHUR. Fine.

HAROLD. Norma and I will pick up the threads again so you mustn't feel bad about me. This is just a temporary withdrawal. (*HE exits through the middle door.*) Just help Norma with my stuff. (*Closes door.*)

(*A slight pause. ARTHUR tries to work.*

*There is the SOUND of someone falling down the
     stairs and a thump against the door.*
*Silence. ARTHUR rises to go and investigate. ROBIN
     enters the French windows carrying a tom-tom
     covered in leopard skin.)*

     ROBIN. It's me again! (*Gives a dazzling smile which
is only slightly embarrassed.)*

(*ARTHUR regards him for the first time, with vague
     interest.)*

     ROBIN. Is this everything, d'you know?
     ARTHUR. Harold will be down in a moment. (*Sits at
his stool and works.)*

(*A pause.)*

     ARTHUR. I've seen you somewhere. You worked
for Harold long?
     ROBIN. Nearly two years.
     ARTHUR. You've been here before, haven't you?
     ROBIN. Once or twice. When Harold comes back
from his trips and has to fly off again after a day or two,
I bring him the office papers to sign. It saves him
traipsing all the way to Luton. Gives him a little
breather at home.
     ARTHUR. Good idea.
     ROBIN. He telexes me from abroad saying when
he's due here and I arrive with all the office papers. He
signs them and I go, then he can relax at home for a
bit.
     ARTHUR. I see. Very lucky for him you should be
leaving your room today.

ROBIN. Yes. It's worked out frightfully well for all parties.

HAROLD. (*Enters from the middle door, carrying an African shield and some spears.*) You got my bongo drums. Good. Shove all this lot in the car, Robin.

ROBIN. Righto, Harold.

(*NORMA enters, carrying a war club.*)

HAROLD. I'll get the war drum.

NORMA. Remember your ligaments, Harold.

ARTHUR. I'll give you a hand.

NORMA. You can take this as well, Mr. Toovey.

ROBIN. Righto, Mrs. Vines.

(*HE takes all the stuff and piles it in the corner as HAROLD and ARTHUR exit.*)

ROBIN. I wasn't sure what that was. It just look like a huge tree trunk.

NORMA. Yes, it's carved out of a tree trunk.

(*As NORMA looks out to the French windows, ROBIN rests his hand discreetly on her bottom. SHE does not move.*)

ROBIN. That a fact? (*HE, too, looks out into the garden.*)

NORMA. He brought it back with him from Africa.

ROBIN. (*His hand moves slightly.*) What does it sound like?

NORMA. (*HER voice wavering slightly.*) Just like someone hitting a hollow tree. (*SHE moves briskly*

*away to the kitchen and busies herself with the
snacks.*)

ROBIN. How's it going? (*Goes over to her.*)

NORMA. (*Glancing out.*) There's a little
complication with Sonia we're sorting it out.

(*ROBIN starts to go through into the kitchen but SHE
lowers the flap.*)

ROBIN. Have I said something?

NORMA. How dare you say my underwear was
tarty! Those French knickers were very expensive!
I've been looking for there everywhere!

ROBIN. I didn't mean for Harold to see them. I
didn't say they were yours! I just said ...

NORMA. That some tart had left them behind! And
who are all these other women you've been having in
the office?

ROBIN. No one! I just say those sort of things to
Harold so he won't suspect about us. Strike me dead!

(*HE darts under the flap and THEY go into a
passionate kiss.*)

NORMA. No really, Robin. Not while my ex-
husband and ex-lover are still on the premises. I
couldn't possibly.

(*SHE keeps a wary eye out to the French windows.
HE stops kissing her.*)

NORMA. We'll be o.k. for two minutes—they've
just gone into the shed.

(*HE kisses the back of her neck. SHE cuts some salmon.*)

NORMA. But I'm not really speaking to you. I didn't think Harold would end up in your lovely room.

ROBIN. I just suggested it on the spur of the moment. I said I was moving in with this dark, sultry, girl with the passionate brown eyes which hint of primitive secrets and nocturnal delights.

NORMA. Oh! That's all right then. (*Gives another careful look out to the French windows.*) You can let yourself in later on, can't you?

ROBIN. I've got my key. (*HE kisses her ear.*)

NORMA. You will try and avoid Arthur for a day or so? When you've got another job, it won't matter who knows ...

(*HE nows adds massaging.*)

NORMA. But I er ... don't want Harold to find out while you're still working for him. You'll get the sack and you know how responsible I feel about you.

(*HE is getting through to her. SHE wants to go but can't.*)

NORMA. Please stop being so wicked, Robin. They'll be coming out of the shed in a minute.

(*THEY disappear below the counter, then come up again.*)

NORMA. NO! I'm serious, Robin. I must think of your mother being a fortnight younger than me. That'll sober me up.

(*THEY embrace again and sink below the counter out of sight.*
ARTHUR *and* HAROLD *enter from the French windows carrying the tree trunk war drum between them.*
NORMA *leans up.* ROBIN *bobs up. SHE pushes him down out of view and keeping her hand on his head—out of sight—SHE sits on the stool and with one hand prepares the sandwiches.*)

ARTHUR. Straight into your car?
HAROLD. Yes, please. (*To Norma.*) Is Robin out there?
NORMA. (*Looks round vaguely.*) He's somewhere about.

(*ARTHUR looks at her.*)

NORMA. My legs went again. I had to sit down.
ARTHUR. If you get this on my shoulder, Harold, I can manage it up the steps and you can collect the rest.
HAROLD. Right.

(*ARTHUR gets the drum on his shoulder and exits. the front door.*)

HAROLD. (*Goes to collect the rest of his kit.*) I'll say cheerio then, Norma.
NORMA. Good bye then, Harold.
HAROLD. (*Crosses down to her.*) No need to look anxious. I really am going.
NORMA. I hope you'll be comfortable in your new place.

HAROLD. It's only one room but it looks over some playing fields. I think they're playing fields.

NORMA. (*Pushes down with one arm.*) Yes, they are.

HAROLD. Pardon?

NORMA. I'm sure they are.

(*HE turns away to pick up the spears. NORMA slaps Robin below the counter.*)

HAROLD. (*Turning back.*) Whatever the future holds, Norma, you know, you'll always have a warm place in my heart.

NORMA. (*An ambiguous groan.*) Oooooooh!

HAROLD. You mind me saying that?

NORMA. Oh no! That's lovely.

HAROLD. Good.

(*HE turns away and SHE kicks Robin below counter.*)

NORMA. Not you!

HAROLD. (*Turns back.*) I'm sorry?

NORMA. That's really nice of you, Harold.

HAROLD. And I'll always be grateful for our first six months together. Happiest time of my life. Our first six months were lovely, weren't they?

NORMA. They were, Harold. Our first SIX ... (*High pitched as SHE reacts to something diabolical happening below.*) ... months ... were heaven, Harold.

HAROLD. Perhaps—when you've had a chance to sort yourself out ... got used to living alone ... perhaps I could take you out for supper.

NORMA. I can't really think straight at the moment

HAROLD. Anyway ... I'll give you a ring sometime. Cheerio, Norma.

(*HE offers her both his hands over the counter. SHE has a daunted moment before SHE takes them, but she has no choice. SHE rises and takes both his hands.*)

NORMA. Cheerio, Harold.
HAROLD. I'll send you my address and telephone number should you ever need me.
NORMA. (*Her eyes roll in horror as SHE reacts to what is going on below.*) Yes, please. Do do that! (*SHE kicks something.*)
HAROLD. I'm sure it won't be ...
NORMA. (*Gives a gurgling sound. Then clears her throat.*) Sorry, Harold, I had a frog in my throat.
HAROLD. I'm sure it won't be too long before we're back together again. I just have a funny feeling.
NORMA. Yes. So do I.

(*ARTHUR enters front door with the war drum still on his back. HE drops it down.
THEY break.*)

ARTHUR. I can't get this pass the gate. We'll take this stuff through Norma's door. Sonia's husband's arriving any minute. He's found out about me and Sonia and I'd rather he didn't see all these spears and African Shillelaghs ... it might give him ideas.
HAROLD. Sorry to hear that. (*Exits followed by Norma.*)

(*As ALL THREE exit carrying something, ROBIN's head appears above the kitchen counter.*

As HE grabs the leopard skin drum, HAROLD appears
    at the middle door.)

HAROLD. Ah there you are, Robin! Arthur wants
us to take the stuff through Norma's flat.
ROBIN. O.k, Harold.

(*THEY go to exit through middle door. A beat.
    DOORBELL.*)

ARTHUR. (*Off.*) Don't answer that! No one answer
that! (*Leaps down the stairs beyond the door and
blocks their way.*) Get out! All of you! Get out
immediately!
HAROLD. We're trying to get out.

(*ARTHUR runs to front door window and takes a peek
    through a slit.
HAROLD and ROBIN go to exit but NORMA appears
    blocking the door.*)

ARTHUR. (*Hoarse whisper.*) It's him!

(*NORMA steps in. ARTHUR grabs her.*)

NORMA. Better open the door then.

(*HAROLD and ROBIN go to exit.*)

ARTHUR. Where you going?
HAROLD. You told us to go.
ARTHUR. I did?
NORMA. We can't involve Harold and Robin.
ARTHUR. No ... no ... But ... he's got a suitcase.
NORMA. A suitcase?

ARTHUR. Why should he arrive with a suitcase?

NORMA. Perhaps he wants to move in.

ARTHUR. They carry tommy guns in suitcases, don't they?

NORMA. That's violin cases.

HAROLD. Look here ... none of your business ... but might I ask ...? Are you expecting some kind of violence from Dennis Bradshaw?

ARTHUR. We're expecting anything.

HAROLD. His case could, in fact, contain something to harm you.

ARTHUR. How do you know?

HAROLD. His company makes ninety-seven percent of Britain's dynamite.

ARTHUR. That's it! He's come to blow me up.

(*The DOORBELL again.*)

ARTHUR. He's got a homemade bomb in that suitcase! That's it! Got to be it! No point in looking on the bright side. I must be prepared for the worst! (*During this HE goes backwards and forwards to the door.*) And he can't have anything worse in that suitcase than a bomb, can he?

NORMA. He could have Sonia's clothes.

ARTHUR. (*Clutches his heart.*) Oh, my God! He's dumping her! Harold ... you go ... but listen behind the curtain; if you think I'm in bad trouble ... rescue me.

HAROLD. How?

ARTHUR. Show yourself. Let him see I'm not all alone.

HAROLD. How do you mean? Show myself?

ARTHUR. Just walk in.

HAROLD. How will I know when to walk in?

ARTHUR. I er ... I er ... when I say Droitwich.
HAROLD. Droitwich? Right!

(*HAROLD and ROBIN back out. NORMA closes the curtain. ARTHUR goes to the front door.*)

ARTHUR. I could have been having a lovely time by now if I hadn't panicked. Every Friday night for the past two years I've always had such a lovely time. (*HE goes to the door.*)
NORMA. Don't argue with him. Whatever he says agree with him.
ARTHUR. I will. (*HE opens the front door. The area is empty. Steps out gingerly; looks up and around. HE comes back and shuts the door happily.*) He's gone. Done a bunk!
NORMA. You sure it was him?
ARTHUR. Of course it was him! Dennis Bradshaw ... the big tycoon ... big shot Bradshaw, but it comes to meeting little Arthur Vines, you can't see him for dust! (*During this HE has poured himself a glass of wine.*) When the chips are down—when it's just me and him face to face ... man to man—whoosh! Collapse of stout party.

(*HE takes a good swig of wine. The DOORBELL rings. HE chokes and sputters.*
NORMA opens the door.
DENNIS BRADSHAW wears a dark grey business suit, but the blue silk hanky in his breast pocket, which matches his Eton tie, gives him a social, leisurely air. He carries a large case.)

NORMA. Dennis Bradshaw, I presume!
DENNIS. Er ... yes.

NORMA. I'm Norma Vines. How exciting to meet you in the flesh at last!

DENNIS. (*Steps in rather overwhelmed with the warmth of her welcome.*) Oh, really! How very charming of you! (*As HE comes in with the case we now see it is made of soft tan leather and there is a distinct bulge in the middle.*)

NORMA. (*Eyes it warily.*) What *have* you brought in that case, Dennis? It's not a bomb is it?

DENNIS. A bomb?!

NORMA. What if it is? If it goes off we'll go together and I can't imagine a more divine way of going because I've been mad about you for years! I never watch Panorama unless you're on it! It's your voice and those little black hairs on the back of your wrist! I've been such a fan of yours and I adored that interview you gave to Ludovic Kennedy. I just had to tell you the moment you arrived.

DENNIS. I'm really most ... Thank you Norma and may I say you are exactly as I imagined. I've heard such a lot about you over the years!

NORMA. (*Mystified.*) You have?

DENNIS. Well naturally.

NORMA. Really?

DENNIS. And if I may return the compliment ... I knew you'd be lovely—I expected that—but I didn't think you'd be as gorgeous as this!

NORMA. (*Flustered, unsure but pleased.*) Really? Is that so?

(*During this ARTHUR has tucked himself in the corner of the kitchen and cannot be seen from the door.*)

DENNIS. (*Looking round.*) So this is where it all goes on, eh? Fascinating! Even more exotic then I imagined!

NORMA. It is?

DENNIS. I expected the leather straps (*Indicates the harness.*) but not the horse's collar. That really is something.. Can't wait to see it in action later!

NORMA. (*Blankly.*) Well, er ... it belongs to a cart ... the shafts go through those rings.

DENNIS. Wonderful! Wonderful! The imagination boggles!

(*HE stops in her perambulation as HE sees ARTHUR about to step into the cupboard.*)

DENNIS. Good evening.

ARTHUR. Good evening.

DENNIS. (*Waits courteously to be introduced. Pause. To Norma.*) Has Arthur nipped out somewhere?

NORMA. That is Arthur.

DENNIS. I'm sorry?!

NORMA. That is Arthur.

DENNIS. Arthur Vines? (*Looks at Arthur in disbelief.*) Your ex-husband?

NORMA. That's right.

(*DENNIS stares at Arthur for a moment then takes out his glasses.*)

ARTHUR. Yes. How are you, Dennis? Very nice of you to pop round. Let's have a drink. Yes, you look exactly as you do on television.

(*DENNIS puts on his glasses and stares at Arthur.*)

ARTHUR. Is it nice being chairman of a large chemical company? Sonia and I are just one day a week. I thought I'd make that clear at the outset— Friday night. That's my position. (*During the above ARTHUR has come out with three glasses of wine on a tray, given one to Norma and ended up facing Dennis.*)

DENNIS. (*Ignores the drink.*) Are you really the chap who has been sleeping with my wife every Friday for the past two years?

ARTHUR. (*His mouth forms several words.*) I don't know how to put it but yes.

DENNIS. Astonishing!

ARTHUR. (*A little put out.*) Astonishing?

DENNIS. You're nothing like I imagined.

ARTHUR. I'm not?

DENNIS. Extraordinary! (*To Norma.*) I imagined Arthur quite differently—from Sonia's description of him.

ARTHUR. She told you what I looked like?

DENNIS. She's always said you reminded her of Marlon Brando.

ARTHUR. Marlon Brando.

DENNIS. I don't wish to be rude but personally ... I can't quite see the resemblance. I hope you're not offended?

ARTHUR. Er ... no ... not at all. I've never *thought* I looked like Marlon Brando! Even when he was in *The Godfather* with all that cotton wool in his cheeks. I've never once thought I looked remotely like Marlon Brando. Mrs. Baldwin in my launderette once said I reminded her of Clint Eastwood.

DENNIS. Sonia never mentioned Clint Eastwood. Always Marlon Brando. (*To Norma.*) Isn't it amazing how we see things in people no one else can?

NORMA. Arthur used to remind me of "The Laughing Cavalier".

DENNIS. (*Takes a step back from Arthur and squints at him.*) I can't see that either.

NORMA. He had a big moustache when we first met.

DENNIS. And yet her description of you, Norma, was very close ... except your mouth is much more tender and sensual.

NORMA. That a fact? (*Wets her lips.*)

DENNIS. Fascinating thing—imagination. (*Sips his wine.*) Is this my Chateau Margaux?

ARTHUR. (*A tiny beat.*) Yes.

DENNIS. My favorite.

ARTHUR. And mine.

DENNIS. (*Takes another sip.*) It travels well.

ARTHUR. It does.

DENNIS. It's very exciting for me to meet you both after such a long time. I've not quite got adjusted to the absence of Marlon Brando, but I'm sure I will as the evening goes on! What made Sonia change her mind?

ARTHUR. Er ...

DENNIS. I've begged her for ages to let me come to your Friday little get-togethers, but she's always said no. Anyway, I'm here now and I'm very pleased and honored to be invited.

ARTHUR. (*Blankly.*) My pleasure.

DENNIS. But just before we begin the high jinks, may I say thank you, Arthur, for giving me a new lease on life.

ARTHUR. (*Cautiously.*) You're most welcome.

DENNIS. And I thank you too, Norma, for your contribution.

NORMA. (*A big social smile. SHE seems to understand.*) Not at all! It was nothing!

ARTHUR. Nothing at all.

DENNIS. You say that, Arthur, because you've never had the slightest trouble that way—according to Sonia—but before she started coming here, I had ten years of it.

NORMA. Ten years? As long as that?

DENNIS. It's been diabolical.

(*ARTHUR behind Dennis mouths "What's he talking about?" to Norma, who is smiling knowingly at Dennis as if she is totally au fait with his conversation.*)

NORMA. You poor thing!

DENNIS. ... one day it's on, the next day it's off. One day you're galloping past the winning post, the next you fall at the first fence and there's a steward's enquiry. You just don't know if you're coming or going.

NORMA. Quite.

DENNIS. I'm even nervous talking about it, and God knows I should be able to talk about it to you Norma! You know all there is to know about me. Why should I feel anxious or ashamed?

NORMA. There's nothing to be ashamed of, Dennis.

DENNIS. I mean if I can't talk to you and Arthur about it ...

NORMA. Who can you talk to about it? Exactly!

(*ARTHUR stares perplexed at Norma.*)

DENNIS. Maybe it's because having imagined you
and Norma and all your friends here on a Friday night
... now I've actually met you I feel a bit shy. We meet as
strangers but intimate strangers. (*Raises his glass.*)
Anyway, to you and Norma. My grateful thanks for
keeping me going so wonderfully! (*He toasts them
and drinks.*)
    ARTHUR. (*Slight pause. Guarded.*) That's very
nice of you, Dennis.
    DENNIS. Especially *last* week. My God! When
Sonia came home last Saturday and told me what all
three of you had got up to ...! (*HE laughs in wondrous
disbelief.*) I nearly had a heart attack! Incredible!

(*HE chuckles at the thought. ARTHUR chuckles.
    NORMA chuckles. Then, as DENNIS turns away
    THEY both mouth their confusion to each other
    till Dennis turns back and nearly catches them.*)

    DENNIS. Quick! I said, (*THEY both jump.*) upstairs
at once. No, really, Norma, what you did to Arthur last
Friday really blew my mind!
    NORMA. (*Smiles.*) Is that a fact?
    DENNIS. I bet you looked wonderful dancing on
that table wearing nothing but that transparent motor
cyclist's outfit!
    NORMA. Er ... when was this, you say, Dennis?
    DENNIS. Last Friday. But perhaps it wasn't that
table?
    NORMA. It could have been. I've had rather a busy
week since then. I can't quite remember.
    DENNIS. And Sonia not only didn't tell me about
your wonderful mouth, she didn't tell me about your
fabulous bum, either!

NORMA. Did she not? (*Her tone getting more refined.*)

DENNIS. Can't wait to see it in action later. (*HE turns to Arthur.*) Is Sonia getting herself ready upstairs?

(*NORMA points her finger to her head to indicate madness to Arthur.*)

ARTHUR. I believe so.

DENNIS. So when she comes down we can get cracking?

ARTHUR. Well, er ... we could ... we, er ... it all depends.

DENNIS. You mean we might give ourselves a little warm up first? (*HE makes nudging secretive gestures.*)

ARTHUR. Er ... anything is possible ... er ... our arrangements for this evening are quite fluid.

DENNIS. Before we do ... something I've been dying to ask you for ages—how do you think these things up?

ARTHUR. Not too sure myself.

DENNIS. Do you give him ideas, Norma?

NORMA. Occasionally.

DENNIS. They don't always work for me.

ARTHUR. Sorry to hear that.

DENNIS. When Sonia tells me what you do—

ARTHUR. She tells you?

DENNIS. Naturally.

ARTHUR. Naturally ... go on.

DENNIS. I rush out and buy all the kit, but it doesn't always do the trick. Mind you, your Moulin Rouge evening was wonderful.

ARTHUR. Moulin Rouge?

DENNIS. You know ... Sonia dressed as a French sailor and you as Toulouse Lautrec whacking her with birch twigs.

NORMA. Birch twigs, Arthur!

(*ARTHUR gestures total ignorance.*)

DENNIS. Sensational! (*To Norma.*) 'And as for you, Norma, doing the can-can with no drawers! (*Roars with lewd laughter.*) Have you anything like that in mind for tonight?

NORMA. It hadn't occurred to me so far, I must confess. At least not tonight. I don't think my legs are quite up to it.

DENNIS. Just that when you phoned, I wasn't quite sure what the flavor of the evening would be ... (*Collects his case.*) ... so I just bunged in a miscellaneous assortment. (*Puts case on table.*) I left my lobster basket in my boot.

ARTHUR. You've got a lobster basket in your boot?

DENNIS. I'm on a single yellow line. Is that o.k.?

NORMA. Yes. At this time of night.

DENNIS. I thought you might be doing the Singapore lobster basket. I've brought my own ropes and pulleys but I see you've got your own ropes. We could use your ropes and my basket, perhaps?

ARTHUR. Perhaps we could. You're the guest.

(*DENNIS puts case on table and undoes it. Then stops.*)

DENNIS. Or are we waiting for Sonia?

ARTHUR. No, we're waiting for you actually.

DENNIS. I'll kick off then?

ARTHUR. Please.

DENNIS. I thought a Genghis Khan outfit might start the ball rolling.

(*As HE rummages within, NORMA, with a terrible fascination, edges to behind his shoulder to get a better look.*
DENNIS, unaware, suddenly brings out a great furry thing which hits her in the face.
SHE leaps away with a piercing scream.)

DENNIS. It's only the hat.

NORMA. Of course. (*Recovers.*) Yes I can see you as Genghis Khan, Dennis. You're a natural for it.

DENNIS. Actually I brought it along for Arthur.

ARTHUR. Me?

DENNIS. (*Hands him hat.*) Sonia said you were very into Genghis Khan.

ARTHUR. Yes ... well. I am some days.

DENNIS. It goes ... with the ... (*Rummages.*)

(*NORMA gets nearer again.*)

DENNIS. ... furry loin cloth. (*HE produces it.*)

NORMA. It would do. It's a two piece, of course.

(*DENNIS hands it to NORMA who hands it to Arthur as if it's a dead rat. ARTHUR holds it up to himself.*)

DENNIS. Your size?

ARTHUR. Yes ... this could be quite snug—'specially if we get another cold snap.

DENNIS. (*Smiles politely as HE searches in the case.*) And the whip, of course. (*HE brings out an object wrapped in tissue paper and waggles it at Norma.*) You like the whip, don't you Norma:

NORMA. Well ... you know? (*Nervously fingering her pearls.*) Not all the time ... I mean ... that is ... some days ... I can take it or leave it.

DENNIS. Marvellous thing about you, Norma—if I may say—you're so cool and elegant—such a lady ... no one would ever believe what you get up to on a Friday night. Do try my Genghis Khan, Arthur. I'd be so flattered.

ARTHUR. Try it now?

DENNIS. Only a suggestion. I wouldn't dream of telling a couple of experts like you how to suck eggs. And I thought you might find this amusing, Norma. (*Produces a plastic garment.*) It's only a little thing but it might appeal.

ARTHUR. I'm glad she hasn't been left out.

DENNIS. I just bought a few items to make a contribution to the evening.

(*HE hands it to NORMA who takes it on the end of one of Harold's drum sticks.*)

NORMA. How kind of you, Dennis. You really shouldn't have bothered! How sweet of you! What exactly ...?

DENNIS. It's a wet-look PVC jumpsuit. Very similar to the open crotch PVC cat suit you wore last week, I should imagine.

NORMA. Oh yes! I was getting a bit bored with that.

DENNIS. It goes with the chains and padlocks, of course. (*HE produces these and spreads them out on the sofa.*)

NORMA. That's why I didn't recognize it at first.

DENNIS. I'll get into my togs then. So you saw my interview with Ludovic Kennedy did you, Norma? (*HE takes off his jacket and undoes his tie.*)

NORMA. I did! Most certainly. I ... (*Eyes him undressing.*) ... was rivetted by it.

DENNIS. Oh good. He tried to catch me out on the problems with the Gateshead plant.

NORMA. But you were in total command the whole time.

DENNIS. Awfully nice of you. I had to make it clear that the redundancies were the result of a global recession in phosphate manufacture. I wasn't to blame nor was it the fault of our Gateshead people. Did I look flustered?

NORMA. Never. Not once.

DENNIS. Good. (*Undoes his waistcoat and puts it neatly over the back of a chair.*) This whole business of labor relations—such an emotive subject. So difficult to avoid the emotional undertones. (*Slips off his shoes.*) Especially when one remembers that many of today's union leaders were conditioned by their fathers' telling them about the Jarrow hunger marches ...

(*HE takes off his trousers then becomes aware that NORMA and ARTHUR are still holding their garments and totally immobile. HE slowly them neatly over the chair.*)

DENNIS. Anything wrong, Arthur?

ARTHUR. (*Snaps out of his stunned trance.*) No! no!

DENNIS. You don't like the loin cloth?

ARTHUR. I do! I love it! Wonderful!

DENNIS. Do try it! I'd be so flattered if it did do something for you. I know I'm only an amateur compared to you but ...

ARTHUR. It's great! (*Puts it on.*) Yes it's really er ... very sort of ooooh, yes ... very Genghis Khanish. Oh, yes! It's definitely doing something for me!

(*HE does a swagger, then catches NORMA's look and turns away sheepishly.*)

DENNIS. How interesting! You're going to wear it *over* your trousers! Intriguing!

ARTHUR. (*Reasonably.*) Thought I would—just to ring the changes.

DENNIS. You're the master. (*Sits and takes off his socks.*) No, that's the basic trouble with these face-to-face interviews on television. (*Puts his socks neatly with his shoes.*) One is always aware that one's answers must be kept simple. (*HE takes out a navy blue skirt from the case and puts it on.*) ... and because of that, it is inevitable that a certain amount of distortion comes into it.

(*HE brushes a fleck of fluff from the skirt then becomes aware that NORMA is still holding up the PVC garment.*)

DENNIS. If you don't fancy the jumpsuit, Norma, I've also brought you a see-through boiler suit. (*From the case HE produces a transparent polythene-like suit with legs and cut-out bosom circles.*) Perhaps this is more to your liking. I know what a creature of moods you are.

NORMA. Very chic! (*Holds it up to herself.*) What do you think, Arthur? Bit too Sloaney for me I'll try it later.

DENNIS. Of course. You slip into it when the urge takes you. Yes, I've appeared half a dozen times this year alone ... BBC ... ITV ...

NORMA. *World at One.*

DENNIS. The lot ... discussing various aspects of the chemical manufacturing industry ... (*He takes out a pair of black stockings and shakes them out ... then searches the case.*) I'm missing something.

NORMA. That's what I was thinking.

DENNIS. M'mm? Ah, no! Garters! (*Produces red garters.*) ... and each time, when the program is over ... (*Sits and puts on the stockings and garters.*)... I always get the feeling that my answers have given an over-simplified view of the problems. You mention *World at One,* Norma, well when Robin asked me why I bought my potash from Germany, I answered as succinctly as I could, tried to avoid getting too technical, but afterwards, when I was relaxing with him in his dressing room having a scotch, I was aware, once again, that I had over-simplified the problem. (*Rises and gets a pair of women's black shoes from the case, returns to the sofa and realizes he's been sitting in front of the Genghis Khan boots.*) Your boots, Arthur. So sorry. (*Hands them to Arthur.*)

ARTHUR. Thanks. I was wondering where they were.

(*As DENNIS puts on the shoes, ARTHUR gingerly puts on the boots.*)

DENNIS. I suppose my traffic warden kit must seem quite tame to you and Norma.

NORMA. Not to me, Dennis. I don't know about Arthur. I was married to him for over 20 years but you never really get to know someone do you?

ARTHUR. (*Sharply.*) What's that mean?! (*To Dennis.*) I'm really fascinated by your traffic warden, Dennis. We haven't had a traffic warden down here for ages. Not a lady traffic warden that is. A lady traffic warden who is a man, I mean. No, we haven't had one of those down here for ... I can't remember the last time. No, it's really great, Dennis.

DENNIS. You're just being kind. You two won't think it's anything to write home about, ... but it has worked out very well for me lately ... (*Takes a lady traffic warden's jacket and puts it on.*) ... so if it does the trick ...

ARTHUR. Why not stick to it? Eh, Norma?

NORMA. Well navy blue has never been quite my color, but it looks very nice on you, Dennis.

DENNIS. Thank you. (*Taking out two long yellow armbands.*) Shall I wear these you think?

ARTHUR. What are they?

DENNIS. Armbands. You need them when you're directing traffic.

ARTHUR. How can you direct down here Dennis?

DENNIS. (*Coughs.*) Don't be ridiculous Arthur! You are a card! No! No! Normally I'd only wear them on point duty outside.

ARTHUR. Quite honestly, Dennis ... I don't want to cramp your style ... live and let live is my motto—it takes all types to make a world but if you're going to go out in the street like that and direct traffic ... there might be a few accidents.

DENNIS. You're quite an amusing chap, d'you know that? Sonia never told me you had this quirky sense of humor. (*Chuckles.*) Very droll. Me directing the traffic like this!

ARTHUR. I mean it!

DENNIS. No, please ... don't make me laugh. This skirt is a bit tight. (*Puts on a black tie which clips to his collar.*) Mind you, all joking aside, I don't know how much longer the meter maid will work for me. (*Swirls.*)

NORMA. But it makes you look ten years younger! Such a lovely swing from the hips!

DENNIS. (*Disinterested.*) Really? Anyway credit where it's due, it's lasted longer than my sado-bondage or my female domination with rubber wet suit.

NORMA. (*Polite small talk.*) And it really does a lot for you, Dennis.

DENNIS. It does! It does! I have to admit my present cross dressing into female authoritative has given me a very good innings .

NORMA. If I wore that no one would give me a second glance.

DENNIS. (*Abstractedly yanks up the top of his stocking.*) Yes, it's a funny business. I wouldn't give you a "thank you" now for an evening with M and S.

NORMA. (*Blankly.*) Would you not?

DENNIS. But I was forgetting, you still have an old fashioned affection for M and S don't you, Norma?

NORMA. (*Pleased that she is picking up the lingo.*) Oh yes! I love Marks and Spencers.

(*During this DENNIS rummages for something in the case.*)

ARTHUR. (*Sotto.*) Masochism and sadism.

NORMA. Who? Oh,God! Really?

DENNIS. (*Taking out an elegant designer carrier bag.*) Is there a mirror I can use, Arthur?

ARTHUR. (*Pulls aside the bathroom curtain.*) Bathroom's at the end of this passage.

DENNIS. Won't be a tic. (*HE exits.*)

(*ARTHUR draws back the curtain as NORMA runs to the middle door. ARTHUR blocks her way.*)

NORMA. I don't think I can help you any more with Dennis.

ARTHUR. (*Urgent, sotto.*) You can't leave me alone with him!

NORMA. I'm very sorry, Arthur, but I don't think I can make any useful contribution. I didn't know about this.

ARTHUR. Nor did I!

NORMA. I had no idea all this was going on down here every Friday.

ARTHUR. You think I did?

NORMA. You're perfectly entitled to do this sort of thing in your own home, but include me out.

ARTHUR. What are you talking about?

NORMA. (*Walks away from door.*) I pass no moral judgement. If you enjoy this sort of thing and don't harm anyone else ...

ARTHUR. (*Crosses down to her.*) I don't know anything about this sort of thing. This is all total news to me!

(*Having got him away from the door SHE runs up to it and flings back the curtain but HE throws the fur hat at her. SHE screams and leaps onto a chair pulling up her skirt.*)

*HE crosses to her, picks up the furry hat and
    threatens her with it.)*

    ARTHUR. If anyone is going, it'll be me!
    NORMA. Please, Arthur—you know I can't stand
little furry things.
    ARTHUR. (*Threatens her with hat.*) How would you
like this crawling up your legs?
    NORMA. (*Terrified.*) Please, Arthur! I'll have
nightmares for a month.
    ARTHUR. Dennis is not dangerous. Years ago I did
the jacket of a medical book called *A History of Sexual
Behavior in Western Society.*
    ARTHUR. I had to read about these kinky people
before I could do the design. They just dress up for a
mental thrill.It's all in the head.
    NORMA. Nowhere else?
    ARTHUR. Correct. There's obviously been a
severe breakdown of communications between me
and Sonia but if we play our cards right, Sonia and I
might be able to resume our normal service next
Friday. So just go along with it and pretend you're as
barmy as he is.
    NORMA. I'm not sure I ...

*(ARTHUR suddenly thrusts the hat back at her. SHE
    screams.)*

    NORMA. I'll stay.

*(There is a tugging behind the bathroom curtain as
    DENNIS tries to open it from the wrong end.)*

DENNIS. (*Behind curtain*.) I heard Norma screaming! So glad you've started on your own. (*Emerging*.) I was feeling a bit inhibited.

(*DENNIS now wears a women's wig which is in the style of a respectable matron. HE has drawn on two, arched eyebrows—his only concession to female make-up. HE wears the yellow armbands, a black leather shoulder bag and carries the usual black, flip-over book of parking tickets. During the following moments HE checks his tickets and the plastic bags in his bag.*
NORMA and ARTHUR both stare at him, then NORMA makes a sound which indicates a smothered guffaw.
ARTHUR glares at her. SHE controls herself, but the effort begins to freeze her features.
A pause.
SHE lets out a tiny, high-pitched squeak. ARTHUR looks back at her instantaneously. SHE makes no further sound, but is obviously in some difficulty as SHE goes with tiny, careful paces, to the bathroom.)

ARTHUR. The bathroom window is locked for the winter.

NORMA. Just ... (*Controls her voice*.) ... toilet! (*SHE exits behind bathroom curtain*.)

DENNIS. I decided on the armbands after all.

ARTHUR. It all helps to ring the changes, doesn't it?

DENNIS. You and Normal sounded as if you had started the evening with the Outraged Husband.

ARTHUR. Outraged husband?

DENNIS. Invented by that German couple in California.

ARTHUR. That's right. The Outraged Husband. That's what we're playing.

DENNIS. Well you ought to know, Arthur. You're the expert.

ARTHUR. Er ...

DENNIS. You start whipping Norma and I rush in.

ARTHUR. Oh, that one. Ah Yes! Of course, it's coming back to me. Where would you like to rush in from?

DENNIS. (*Glances in at the open bedroom door.*) The bedroom?

ARTHUR. Be my guest.

DENNIS. When I hear the whipping ...

DENNIS. Do you want to use your own whip?

ARTHUR. Er ...

DENNIS. Or this harness? (*He lifts up the harness straps.*) You could give her a good thrashing with this.

ARTHUR. Er ...

DENNIS. You're most welcome to use my whip. (*He offers Arthur the whip still wrapped in tissue paper.*)

ARTHUR. (*Taking it.*) I will. Make an interesting change.

DENNIS. So you whip her and I burst in and catch you at it. O.k.?

ARTHUR. Got it! You burst in ... catch us at it and then ...er ... then er ...

(*DENNIS opens the parking ticket book and takes off a pen attached by an elastic band.*)

ARTHUR. Ah! I see. You give us both parking tickets!

DENNIS. Parking tickets?

ARTHUR. I'm with you.

DENNIS. (*Seriously troubled.*) I don't usually give you both parking tickets.

ARTHUR. Just give me one then. Am I on a double or a single yellow line?

DENNIS. Don't know. Up to now I haven't taken it that far. You've got me a bit worried now.

ARTHUR. No! No! I'll leave it up to you ... just so long as you don't produce any wheel clamps. (*Laughs.*)

DENNIS. You'll have to help me ... over this, Arthur. Sonia never told me about parking tickets or wheel clamps.

ARTHUR. No ... well you just do what you normally do at home.

(*NORMA comes out of the bathroom. SHE wears a translucent shower cap, a plastic "Y" shaped hose—normally used for washing hair—round her middle as a belt and Arthur's old slippers.*)

DENNIS. I say! The fun's beginning to start!

NORMA. Just thought I'd get in the mood.

DENNIS. Not half! So you both want parking tickets?

ARTHUR. Forget the parking tickets.

DENNIS. Right. I'll give you time to warm up ...

ARTHUR. Then you burst in.

DENNIS. (*Chuckling, goes to the bedroom, slapping Norma's bottom on the way.*) Wunderbar! (*HE exits into bedroom. Door shuts.*)

NORMA. (*Goes to Arthur.*) I've been thinking, Arthur. (*Furtive whisper.*) No doubt about it, Dennis has got some kind of nervous trouble.

(*ARTHUR begins to unwrap the whip.*)

NORMA. At first, I thought it was our phone call which suddenly triggered it off, but I think he must have been a bit odd before we phoned!

(*ARTHUR cracks the whip. NORMA jumps.*)

ARTHUR. I've got to pretend to whip you.

(*Cracks whip a little nearer to Norma. SHE yelps.*)

ARTHUR. (*Shouts towards bedroom door.*) Take that, you bitch!

(*Cracks whips close to Norma. SHE backs nervously to the door.*)

NORMA. Don't get carried away, Arthur.
ARTHUR. (*As before.*) Outraged! I'll give you bloody outrage! I'm going to thrash the arse off you!

(*HE cracks the whip. NORMA goes to the French windows. HE stops her progress with another crack of the whip. HE runs to the French windows and locks them. Puts the key in the hat and puts it on.*)

ARTHUR. Take that!

(*Cracks whip. NORMA leaps and screams. HE advances on her. SHE holds up a cushion to protect herself.*)

NORMA. Please don't, Arthur ... I would never have asked you to get rid of Harold if I'd known it would lead to this.

(*HE cracks the whip. SHE yelps and throws the harness at him.*)

NORMA. This is beyond a joke, Arthur! I mean it!

(*Cracks the whip. SHE gives a real scream of pain.*)

ARTHUR. (*Quietly and conversationally.*) That was very good, Norma.
NORMA. Because you hit me!

(*HE circles round the room with the whip raised. SHE backs.*)

NORMA. Don't you dare lay another finger on me!
ARTHUR. Take that, you whore! (*Cracks whip and laughs maniacally.*) You dirty little tart!

(*Cracks whip again. NORMA picks up the horse's collar to defend herself.*
DENNIS bursts out of the bathroom behind her.)

DENNIS. (*His normal voice but angry.*) You bloody swine!

(*DENNIS sounds so genuinely angry that ARTHUR freezes on the spot.*
HE throws her down on the sofa as if protecting her. NORMA's head goes through the collar. Everyone is transfixed for three seconds.)

(*NORMA and ARTHUR are transfixed for a second.*)

ARTHUR. I'm terribly sorry.
DENNIS. How dare you? (*A beat.*) I'm talking to
you! You perverted pig!

(*ARTHUR searches for a clue.*)

DENNIS. (*Loud whisper.*) You say "she likes it!"
ARTHUR. Sorry! She likes it! Tell him Norma.

(*DENNIS acts "astonishment" in an over-the-top
    amateur fashion. HE remains totally masculine
    with nothing feminine in voice or gesture.*

DENNIS. My wife likes it? (*Turns "outraged" to
Norma and tosses the collar away ash HE bring her to
her feet.*) You dirty little bitch!

(*NORMA slaps his face immediately. ARTHUR is
    appalled.*)

NORMA. Oh, dear! So sorry!
DENNIS. (*Normal bland manner.*) I loved it. You're
so much better at it than Sonia.
NORMA. Thank you. How kind.
DENNIS. (*Resumes his role.*) She likes it, you say?
ARTHUR. (*Hesitates.*) I think so. Er ... yes! Yes,
she does!

(*HE cracks the whip at no one in particular.*)

NORMA. I don't! I don't! (*SHE backs, genuinely
nervous.*)

DENNIS. Ah, yes! I see exactly what's been going on while I was in Frankfurt! (*Goes slowly to Norma.*) So you like it, eh?

NORMA. (*Backing.*) Well – you know? It depends on the weather. Some times I hate it.

DENNIS. You hate it, eh?

NORMA. More than likely.

DENNIS. (*Suddenly to Arthur.*) You know what this means? (*Pause.*) Do you?

ARTHUR. I'll have to square with you, Dennis. At this moment, I don't know what day it is.

DENNIS. (*Roaring.*) She's been making a monkey out of you!

ARTHUR. Me?

DENNIS. That lying slut has been laughing at us!

ARTHUR. (*Leaps on this and strides to Norma with the whip raised.*) Is this true?

DENNIS. Don't *talk* to her. Give her a lash!

(*ARTHUR cracks the whip. NORMA leaps and yelps clutching her bottom.*)

NORMA. No! It's not true!

DENNIS. Again!

NORMA. It's not true!

DENNIS. Him, not you!

NORMA. Oh, sorry.

(*ARTHUR cracks the whip.*)

DENNIS. She's got to admit it! Admit it! You double-crossing little whore!

(*ARTHUR cracks the whip.*)

NORMA. (*Cowering tearfully.*) It might be true.

ARTHUR. What do I do now?

DENNIS. Do? Do!! There's only one sort of medicine she understands!

(*DENNIS grabs Norma and puts her across his knee.*)

NORMA. No! No! You bastard!

(*HE spanks her once. SHE yells.*)

DENNIS. You know you love it, Norma. (*Spanks her once.*)

NORMA. I hate it!

DENNIS. You hate it and love it ... (*Smack.*) ... love it and hate it! You've got to have it!

NORMA. Stop it! Stop it!

DENNIS. Medicine and discipline. Heil Hitler!

ARTHUR. I'll put on the Wagner. (*HE turns up to the cassette and puts on "Ride of the Valkyries."*)

NORMA. Get him off, Arthur! Get this mad bastard off!

(*ARTHUR cracks the whip in time.*)

SONIA. (*At the crescendo of screams, SONIA enters the front door.*) Oh, my God!

(*Everything stops. SONIA closes the door leaving her bunch of keys in the lock. ARTHUR turns off the music.*)

DENNIS. (*Smiles urbanely.*) Hello, darling. (*HE courteously helps Norma to her feet.*) We thought a little warm up would break the ice ... as I've never met this charming couple. A most enjoyable start to the evening, don't you agree?

ARTHUR. I do and we've certainly gotten to know each other.

SONIA. How did you get here?

DENNIS. By car, of course.

SONIA. I was waiting on the corner for you by Fulham Road.

DENNIS. I came along the Old Brompton Road.

SONIA. It's much quicker by the Fulham Road.

DENNIS. Does it matter?

SONIA. I was hoping to stop you. I wanted to explain. I knew you had left because there was no answer when I phoned.

DENNIS. Well, naturally! I wasn't going to waste a moment. My first invitation! I was so thrilled! I do wish you had allowed me to meet them earlier!

SONIA. I thought it better you didn't.

DENNIS. Well not every Friday, I agree, but once in two years can't do anyone any harm! I did so much want to thank Norma and Arthur for rejuvenating my life the way they have. (*A radio PHONE rings.*) Pardon me! (*HE goes to his case and takes out a radio phone and speaks into it.*) Bradshaw. I don't believe it. Yes. Telex affirmative and get me on the next Concorde to New York or direct to Minnesota. I'll be at London airport in 40 minutes. Phone me boarding instructions en route. (*Hangs up.*) Awfully sorry. I must leave immediately. (*Starts undressing.*) If I can be in Minnesota ten a.m. their time tomorrow to sign the contract, I can get half a million pounds worth of tetrachloric diasulphate dirt cheap.

SONIA. You must go, Dennis!

DENNIS. I must!

(*SONIA helps HIM undress.*)

DENNIS. It'll be the biggest bargain I've picked up for years. Sorry to leave you lin the lurch like this.

ARTHUR. Business before pleasure, Dennis. (*HE, too, begins to help DENNIS undress.*)

NORMA. It's been wonderful meeting you. (*SHE, too, helps him undress.*) Short but wonderful.

DENNIS. And we will meet again I hope?

SONIA. We'll discuss it when you get back.

ARTHUR. I don't think I could manage next Friday.

(*DENNIS puts on his trousers. SONIA holds his tie. ARTHUR puts on his socks.*)

ARTHUR. Certainly not. Mustn't take the gilt off the gingerbread. I'll give you a ring next year perhaps.

DENNIS. Would you, really? It's been marvellous meeting you, Arthur. It's such a comfort to find someone even kinkier than oneself. (*HE is now dressed.*) You'll take my kit home tomorrow won't you, Sonia?

SONIA. I will.

DENNIS. If Arthur gets his hands on it, I'll never see it again. (*HE laughs and shakes hands with Arthur.*) Wonderful evening, Arthur. (*Kisses Norma chastely on the cheek.*) So thrilled to meet you, Norma.

(*ARTHUR opens the front door for Dennis. DENNIS turns at the door.*)

DENNIS. And will you cancel my meeting in Droitwich tomorrow, Sonia?

ARTHUR. (*Suddenly.*) Droitwich!

(*HAROLD and ROBIN enter chanting and dancing, carrying the African instruments. HAROLD is dressed as an Arab with the aid of sheets. HE leads ROBIN who wears only a leopard skin. Round his ankles are two raffia lampshades.*)

DENNIS. Oh dear! What delights I'm missing. I knew all the time you had something extraordinary up your sleeve! I do so hate to leave you! (*Exits.*)

(*ARTHUR shuts the door. Gradually THEY stop playing.*)

SONIA. He's still got his eyebrows on.

(*ARTHUR opens the door and looks up. Sound of CAR driving off. HE closes the door.*)

ARTHUR. Perhaps the air hostess will tell him.
NORMA. If not, he'll go all the way to Minnesota in those raised eyebrows.
ARTHUR. It could do him some good. The Yanks might take one look at his outraged expression and lower the price. I would. Those eyebrows terrified the life out of me!

(*A slight pause. Gradually THEY look at HAROLD and ROBIN, who shuffle, uneasily.*)

ARTHUR. What are you two going as?
HAROLD. Well, we heard snatches of chat about whips and bondage, so I thought I'd be a slave trader and Robin the slave.
ARTHUR. A most commendable effort.

rates next week.

ROBIN. Did we fit the bill?

HAROLD. We gathered that fancy dress was the order of the day, so I borrowed a pair of your sheets, Norma.

NORMA. I recognize them.

HAROLD. Did we serve some good purpose?

ARTHUR. You didn't do much for me, but I think you got Dennis going. I thought I was going to have to throw a bucket of cold water over him.

NORMA. I think Arthur and Sonia would like to be alone for a moment.

HAROLD. Of course.

ROBIN. Naturally.

(*ALL THREE exit middle door.*)

ARTHUR. So you invented Monica's restaurant just for my benefit?

SONIA. (*Begins to pick up the clothes and pack them.*) I had to give *you* some reasonable explanation for Dennis allowing me to spend every Friday night away from home.

ARTHUR. And when you got back Saturday morning?

SONIA. I made up these fantasies about you to try and help Dennis's ailment.

ARTHUR. Your inventions? Or did you look them up in the three volume edition of *A History of Sexual Behavior in Western Society?*

SONIA. Who told you that?

ARTHUR. I recognized some of the fantasies. There's this ex-police sergeant in Vancouver who occasionally directs traffic dressed as a lady Mountie. He was very good at it apparently. He had been directing traffic for twenty years as a man and he thought he needed a change. I did the book jacket.

SONIA. I didn't know. I'm sorry if I've upset you.

ARTHUR. What upsets me is that you didn't recognize my book jacket!

SONIA. I should have known at once! Your style is so distinctive. So clever of you to use Greek mythology ... Cupid and Psyche.

ARTHUR. (*Sulking.*) It was her mother-in-law—Aphrodite. Aphrodite and Hermes, with a few water nymphs.

SONIA. Did Aphrodite have a thing with Hermes?

ARTHUR. She does in my version. So for the past two years you've been using me as some kind of weirdo sexual symbol.

SONIA. Not you—just volume one.

ARTHUR. So when he arrived he thought it was me who put you in a lobster basket every Friday?

SONIA. That is what I had led him to believe ... yes.

ARTHUR. And it was me who pulled you up to the ceiling in the basket with the aid of pulleys, then lowered you, with me on the floor pulling the ropes as in Chapter Six I believe?

SONIA. Chapter Seven. Some people in Kidderminster do that.

ARTHUR. And I suppose he chose the wine?

SONIA. Yes.

ARTHUR. When you first met me ...

SONIA. I'll never forget the day you came into my office ...

ARTHUR. It's too late to chat me up. When I walked into your office ...

SONIA. I was looking for some fantastic lover I could tell Dennis about in order to try and cure his little problem.

ARTHUR. And you found me?

SONIA. Yes. At first I used to tell him what we did, but after a time he said you were too ordinary for him.

ARTHUR. I'm sorry to be so dull.

SONIA. But you suited me beautifully; but then I fell in love. That was not in my agreement with Dennis. So I decided that either I must give you up ...

ARTHUR. Or buy *A History of Sexual Behavior* in three volumes? Why didn't you tell me before?

SONIA. I knew you'd be cross. I couldn't risk losing you. (*To Arthur.*) Shall I go home now?

ARTHUR. You might as well stay, since it's Friday.

(*SONIA exits into bedroom.*
ARTHUR tidies the room. A car is heard driving off.
HE looks up out of the basrment window .
PHONE rings.)

ARTHUR. (*Into phone.*) Hello? Yes Norma I know Harold and Robin have just left. Yes, I also know you've been having an affair with Robin which is why you wanted me to get rid of Harold. Juliet told me. Yes, she said you had sworn her to secrecy but there you are—she's her daddy's girl. Why did I still do it to Harold? I have no explanation. My feelings are very mixed. Where you're concerned —as ever—but I wish you well with your young man. (*He hangs up, then turns off the LIGHTS and opens the bedroom door.*)

ARTHUR. So, apart from the electrical socket, you had quite a good week, did you? (*HE enters. Door shuts.*)

CURTAIN

PROPERTY LIST

ACT I

<u>On Stage:</u>

Coffee table.

Desk. On it: artist's materials, anglepoise type lamp, half finished design for book jacket, electric pencil sharpener, Arthur's glasses.

Built-in bookshelves with cassette player and book.

Easy chair.

Two kitchen stools.

Kitchen counter with entrance.

Kitchen with basic kitchen equipment including electric kettle, packet of cornflakes.

Kitchen cupboard: In it: Ewbank type carpet sweeper, ironing board and iron.

Norma's door screened by curtain concealing miscellaneous bric-a-brac including blanket, garlic squeezer and grip.

Arthur's mac hanging up on hook.

Wastepaper basket.

Various items of clothing and used crockery spread around.

Lead Cupid glimpsed out in patio.

<u>Off Stage:</u>

Plastic bag containing laundry including white shirt dyed half pink.

Grip with duty free bag containing bottle of Southern Comfort and box of cigars.(Harold)

Cardboard box of groceries including whole salami, smoked salmon, cheese and wine. (Sonia)

<u>Personal</u>

Piece of paper (Norma)

Hanky (Harold)

Handbag (Sonia)

ACT II

Flat very tidy.
Strike: all Arthur's strewn clothing.
Set:Duster
On Stage:
Plate of cocktail snacks (Norma)
Off Stage:
Bottle of Southern Comfort (Harold)
Various African tribal warfare items such as drum and
    leopard skin outfit (Robin)
African spears (Norma)
Suitcase (Dennis) In it: Ghenghis Khan-type fur hat,
    boots and spurs, leather straps with chains and
    locks, fur loincloth, whip, female traffic warden's
    outfit, red garters, shoulder bag with book of
    parking tickets and pen, PVC jumpsuit, portable
    radio phone.
Female spectacles (Dennis)
Personal:
Glasses (Dennis)

LIGHTING PLOT

ACT I: Anglepoise lamp and two or three table lights.
    Anglepoise switched on when Arthur works at
    desk. Other lamps not on.
ACT II: Evening. Later that day: Table lamps on at
    beginning for early evening lighting.